CHRISTMAS COLLECTION
THREE HEARTWARMING FESTIVE NOVELLAS

MELISSA HILL

Copyright © Little Blue Books, 2021

The right of Melissa Hill to be identified as the Author of the Work has been asserted by her in accordance with the Copyright, Designs and Patents Act 1988.

All rights reserved. No part of this publication may be reproduced, stored in a retrieval system, or transmitted, in any form or by any means without the prior written permission of the author. You must not circulate this book in any format.

All characters in this publication are fictitious and any resemblance to real persons, living or dead is purely coincidental.

THE CHRISTMAS ESCAPE

CHAPTER 1

*L*ibby Pearson woke with a smile on her face.

It was a couple of weeks to Christmas and already she could feel magic in the air. She leapt out of bed and hurried into the shower to get ready for work.

She was one of the few people she knew who actually liked getting up to go to the office every day - adored her job and the certain thrill that came with walking into Jefferson & Jacobs Marketing.

Her hair was dark and damp as she slipped her arms in the sleeves of her new red jacket, which matched the pencil skirt she was wearing. Her blouse was white with an oversized collar and cuffs that folded over the ends of the jacket, and she wore black and white polka dot heels to match her bag.

"Morning Mom and Dad," she said with a smile as in the living room she passed photos of her parents on the mantle over the fireplace.

Libby always went the long way to the kitchen just to say good morning to them each day. Her parents passed away six years ago. Her father had a heart attack and just one day after he died, her mother went to sleep and didn't wake up.

In the kitchen, the smell of freshly brewed coffee filled her senses and made her feel even happier. She loved coffee in the morning. Food was a second thought, usually something she didn't feel like until lunchtime, but coffee was an absolute must to start the day.

Jingle must've heard her because seconds after she walked into the kitchen, the dog door opened and her friendly, fearless pooch came trotting in. Jingle was a Weimaraner and his stubby tall wagged eagerly at the sight of her.

"Hey boy," she said with a smile as he followed her around the room. "How's it going this morning?"

She poured the coffee into her festive thermal mug, grabbed her lunch from the fridge and packed it into her bag. Libby was trying her best to improve on what she ate, especially so close to the holidays.

She left food for Jingle. He could eat it all and even the bowl too, so she liked to leave a little something extra for him during the day before she gave him his dinner when she got home.

Her parents' house, and forever the Pearson family home was decorated from top to bottom for the season, just like every other house on Clayton Drive.

Nearly every building in the neighbourhood was decorated in hundreds of lights, and those who didn't have hundreds had thousands.

It had taken Libby three days to finish decorating theirs inside and out, but she adored every second of it. Christmas was her favourite time of year and she couldn't imagine it without all the trimmings and festive cheer.

She was barely behind the seat of her little beat-up Fiat

500 when her phone rang. She pressed her Bluetooth button and a second later her brother's voice filled her ears.

"Hey Andy," she greeted as the garage door opened and she began to reverse.

"Sis, don't forget to pick up the turkey," her older brother reminded her. "And you need to make sure to get the cranberries. That canned stuff made Molly itch all night last year."

Her brother's wife was allergic to a great many things, mostly preservatives, so everything had to be made from scratch as Libby had painfully learned last year.

"I remember. I got them up yesterday."

"What about pumpkins? You know how everyone loves your pumpkin and pecan pie," her brother continued.

"I haven't gotten to that yet," she informed him, as she pulled onto the main road and started the journey toward the city. Her office lay at the heart of Rochester's business hub and usually took her about twenty minutes to reach.

"What're you waiting for? You know what the markets will be like the closer to Christmas you get. You risk not getting the good stuff," he brother insisted.

Libby sighed and rolled her eyes. What did Andrew know about markets during the holidays?

In the six years since her parents' passing, Christmas dinner had fallen solely on her shoulders to prepare. She was the one who stood in line at the store to make sure they had all the traditional stuff their mother used to give them.

Though at least her mom had help with the preparations and shopping. Libby had none.

Her phone beeped again and now her sister's name appeared on the screen. "Andy, can you hold? Emma is on the other line."

"OK," her brother replied. "Tell her hi for me and remind

her that Kelsey and Brittany are supposed to come over next weekend for their Brownie campout thing."

"I'll remind her," Libby replied before switching the call. "Hi, Ems."

"Libby, did you get the turkey yet?" her sister asked in a rush.

Why was everyone calling her to ask about a dead bird?

"I got it yesterday," she informed her.

"And the cranberries. Andrew was such a mess last year …"

"Yes, I know. He's actually on the other line and was just telling me the same thing. He also wanted me to remind you about Brit and Kelsey's Brownie camp thing this weekend."

"Right, I almost forgot. Tell him he can drop them at my house for eight. I can give them breakfast before they have to go meet the rest of the troupe."

"Em, why don't you just call and tell him that yourself?" Libby questioned. "You don't need me as an intermediary."

"You're already on the phone with him though," her older sister remarked. "Just tell him what I said OK?"

"Fine." She waited for her sister to continue.

"Well? Aren't you going to tell him?" Emma replied after a moment of silence.

"You meant *now*?" Libby asked incredulously.

"Yes, I want to know what he says."

Libby *really* hated it when her family made her the go-between. Why they didn't just call each other and leave her out of it was beyond her.

She spent the next several minutes playing phone tag with her siblings and listening to them remind Libby of all the things she needed to get done before Christmas.

Story of her life.

CHAPTER 2

When Libby arrived at the office, the cheer had all but left her.

It was one thing for Andy and Emma to call, but then her other sister Megan plus Emma's twin Eden had also phoned to tell her the same things.

It would be nice if instead of ordering me around, even one *of them would maybe help me for once.*

"Not all, but just one would be *very* much appreciated," she muttered to herself as she got out of the car and walked into the building.

Was it her fault she was the only one who was still single and didn't have a spouse or children? Was it her fault she didn't have in-laws coming for a visit?

She wanted to be married and have a family like the next person, but husbands didn't just drop out of the air like snowflakes nor children sprout up from cabbage patches.

Libby walked into the office and was greeted by another example of her yuletide efforts. She'd spent all weekend decorating to make sure the staff had something bright and keeping with the season when they arrived on Monday morning.

"Libby, great work - I can't believe you did this all on your own!" Janice the head accountant said as they passed in the hall. "Let me know next time, I'd love to help."

Colleagues were willing to help her when it came to the office, so why wasn't her own family willing to when it came to a family tradition that had been established long before she was even *born*?

They had enjoyed forty-five years of Pearson Christmases in that house; the first five was just her parents before Andrew joined them.

So why was it that her, with only twenty-six years under her belt with their parents and six without, was charged with carrying on the tradition for the entire family? It didn't seem fair, but then again, whoever said life was when it came to family…

Libby loved this time of year but her siblings were taking it too far. They acted as if she had nothing better to do than prepare everything.

Thank goodness for work. If there was one sure thing that could take her mind off of her worries it was that.

As if on cue, the phone rang and her boss's extension appeared on the display.

"Libby, could you come into my office for a few minutes?"

"Sure thing, Steven, I'll be right there."

That was odd. What did he want that she needed to come into his office? Her mind immediately began to conjure up every conceivable scenario to explain it.

Steven Jefferson was a marketing genius, and one of the main reasons Libby had applied to the company right out of college.

She walked the long corridor to the door on the right.

"Come in," Steven said and Libby quickly turned the handle and entered.

"Morning," she greeted with a smile as she walked over to one of the chairs facing his desk and took a seat.

He smiled at her. "You did a really great job with the office decorating, Libby. I needed to commend you."

He's called her in there to congratulate her on her festive decorating skills? There she was, getting nervous over nothing.

"And since as you did such a great job with the office, I thought you would be the perfect person to pitch Hershell Chocolate's new Christmas campaign."

Libby's eyes almost jumped out of her head. Hershell Chocolate was one of their biggest clients.

"What about Amanda?" Libby asked, referring to the executive who usually handled Hershell.

Steven sighed. "Sadly, Amanda has decided to leave us," he informed. "That means we're in need of another senior marketing exec."

Libby's heart began to leap in her chest. Did this mean he was considering *her* for the job?

"I hadn't heard," she replied as she tried to remain calm.

"We were keeping it under wraps until the time came that we could announce her departure and the new appointment," Steven explained. "So we've asked you and Mark Clarke to come up with a presentation. The one Hershell likes best will be who takes over the account and the rest of Amanda's portfolio. Are you up for it?"

"Yes!" Libby answered a little too eagerly.

Steven laughed. "I like your gusto. You have ten days to prepare for the presentation," he continued as he explained what they were looking for in the new plan, and who would be present for the meeting.

This was quite possibly the biggest thing to happen in Libby's career since the day she was hired.

If she landed this account it could make her at the company. Ten days wasn't a lot of time, but she was sure she could make it happen.

"Thank you for considering me," she said as she got to her feet.

"You're a great worker Libby. We notice that here and we reward the effort we see," Steven replied as he got to his feet to show her out. "I look forward to seeing your pitch."

"I won't let you down," she replied determinedly.

CHAPTER 3

Libby could hardly contain her excitement as she walked back to her office.

She kept looking around to see if anyone was noticing the ridiculously large grin on her face, but they were all busy being productive.

She sat her desk and stifled a squeal of glee at how the morning had turned around. Then her phone disturbed her joy.

"Hey Megan," she said immediately, recognising the number from the display.

"Libby, can you pick up Justin and Julia from school for me today? Ron's parents are arriving later and his car just broke down on the highway so I have to go get them."

"Meg …" she tried to interrupt, but her sister's focus was so honed to her own desires she didn't even hear her.

"They need to be picked up at three and then Justin needs to go to soccer and Julia to dance class."

"Megan, I just got a big project at work. I can't leave the office early today," she protested.

"What? But you're the only person who's close enough to get there on time. What do you want me to do?"

"Maybe call one of their classmate's parents and see if they can?"

"You want to just pass your niece and nephew onto a stranger?" Megan argued.

Libby sighed. Why did they never understand? "Fine. I'll pick them up. I'll just skip lunch and leave early."

"Thanks sis, you're a gem," her sister replied quickly hanging up.

Libby sighed as she held the dead receiver. "So why don't I feel like one …"

CHAPTER 4

Christmas music was playing softly in the background as Libby hummed along.

This truly was the cheeriest time of year, and if all went well, it was going to be even more so for another reason – her promotion.

Her entire career was riding on this one presentation and Libby was determined to nail it.

She'd stayed up late for nights on end trying to come up with a concept, when suddenly it struck her while she was watching *A Muppet Christmas Carol* for the millionth time.

"The Hershell people are going to be blown away," she mumbled happily as she worked.

Since then, her design boards were coming along brilliantly. A few more and she'd have everything ready to print and present. She'd called the Henson company regarding the potential use of muppets, and they agreed to discussing a deal if the client came onboard.

Everything was working out perfectly; all she had to do

was complete and execute it, and the job of new senior marketing executive was all hers.

"Hey Miss Christmas, we were thinking of having a little holiday party on Christmas Eve. What do you say?" her colleague Sharon said as she poked her head around the door to Libby's office.

"I thought we were already having an office party?"

Had something changed and Libby wasn't informed?

"Not here. At my place. Brian and Russel from accounting are down for it. Rob and Joan from printing said they'd join too. And Bobby, Stuart, Leslie and Hailey."

"So I'm the last to know?" Libby mused and Sharon grinned.

"No. I'm just going floor by floor."

"What time?" she asked. Sharon was always looking for a reason to party. She was single, thirty and gorgeous. She had no desire to marry or have a family. She was a career woman with a plan to open her own company in a few years. Libby had no doubt she could do it if only she would get her head out of fun. She spent more time planning events than she did getting her work done.

"Count me in," Libby said with a smile. "I could use some holiday cheer."

Just then her phone rang. It was her sister. Again.

"Hey, Eden."

"Look, I know I said I would pitch in to help you get things ready for Christmas dinner, but I just can't. I am completely swamped. You're going to have to get it done yourself this year, sorry."

"Like every year you mean? Aw, you promised to help this time. It's a lot to do for one person. At least setting up and making dessert would make things easier. I cook the entire meal and clean *and* set up the house…"

"I know, but I really can't. Also, I don't think I'll be able to make dessert either. Adam surprised me with an early Christmas gift and he's taking me to Las Vegas for a few days. We won't be back until Christmas Eve and there's no way after a jaunt like that I'd be able to function."

Libby sighed. There was always a reason more important than helping her.

Eden had one, Andy did … all of her siblings. It was as if they believed their lives were more important than hers.

Still, Libby did it every year because it wouldn't be Christmas otherwise. A day with no turkey, cranberry sauce, yule log and all the other trimmings just wasn't Christmas.

It was an important time for them as a family.

"I guess I'll have to figure it out on my own again," she sighed.

"Forgive me?"

"Don't I always?" she answered as the weight of the additional preparations she had to make began to weigh on her. She could feel a headache coming on.

"That's because you're great. Love you. See you when I get back."

The call ended and Libby was left wondering how this had happened to her yet again. Sharon was still staring at her when she finally came back to her senses.

"Sorry Sharon, but…"

"But you have stuff to do for Christmas. I know. It's always the same with you. Let me guess, one of your sisters flaked on you again?" her friend said as she entered the room and shut the door.

She crossed the floor to the chair on the opposite side of

Libby's desk and sat. Then crossed her legs at the knees and began to strum her perfectly manicured nails on the corner of her desk.

"Why don't you ever just tell them to take a hike and that you're doing something for yourself for a change?" Sharon questioned.

"Because I can't," Libby replied as she picked up some loose papers and moved them from one corner of her desk to the other.

"Why not? You are a thirty-two-year-old puppet. They pull your strings and you do whatever."

"That's not fair," Libby retorted. "It isn't like that."

"Really? What about Thanksgiving?"

Why had she ever told Sharon about that?

It was the day before Thanksgiving. Megan had offered to take on the challenge this year. Everything had been going great until Libby had got a panicked call from her sister telling her how she'd forgotten to defrost the turkey.

She'd burned up the sweet potato mash she'd prepared before time to save her the effort on the day. Everything was going up in flames and she needed Libby's help.

She was always the one to answer the call. She couldn't help it. She was the baby of the family. The one who was always called on to do things whenever her siblings wanted something. It was what she was used to and unfortunately, that hadn't changed in their minds even with the passing of twenty years.

So that day, Libby had left work early. Got into one of the mile-long lines at the butcher shop near her to get a fresh turkey for them to cook. She then went to the market to get the things her sister had wasted before going over to her house to take over the ship.

Megan wasn't used to cooking for so many and she underestimated what it took to prepare for such a big crowd.

Libby also gave up her dinner plans with Todd, the handsome partner from the law firm that occupied the floor below. He'd broken things off with her the day after Thanksgiving. He said she lived her life too much for her family and didn't have time for him.

"I know they're family and you love them, but Libby, there comes a time when you have to tell them 'no'," Sharon was saying now. "One word. Two letters."

"I know how it's spelled," Libby answered.

"I know you know 'I can't' and 'Maybe next time' but honestly, I don't think I've ever heard you say no - at least not to them. Everything is always 'yes'."

"I understand what you're saying," Libby sighed. "I just don't know how to do that. How do you disappoint your family at such a special time of year?"

"I don't know. Why don't you ask yours? They do it to you every year."

Sharon's words hurt. Mostly because they were true and Libby knew it.

"Libby, I hate to be the Grinch to your Cindy Lou Hoo, but maybe it's time for you to take a break from all the Christmas is for other people stuff, and look at having a holiday that *you'd* enjoy for a change. Tell me the truth. When the food is gone and it's time to go home, who's the one *also* left with the cleaning up and rearranging the furniture?"

Libby sat back in her seat and thought about it. The more she thought about it, the more unhappy she became.

She couldn't think of a single time since her parents' death that any of her siblings had stayed back after to help either.

"Me," she finally answered.

"Let me guess. They always have children to get to bed, or a long drive, or some other reason why they can't give you a helping hand." Sharon got to her feet and looked at Libby sadly. "I'm sorry to say it hon, but your siblings don't appreciate you. Maybe it's time you look at doing something for yourself. Take a vacation maybe. Go someplace warm or exotic to get away from this cold, and take a break from the crazy shopping lines and big family Christmas dinners. Just my suggestion."

Libby watched as Sharon left. She was gone but the words she'd spoken remained.

She swiveled in her chair and looked out the window at the falling snow outside.

A vacation from Christmas? It sounded lovely. More than lovely, it sounded like a dream, but there was no way she could do it.

Christmas was about family and togetherness. Libby couldn't just up and leave hers.

Could she?

CHAPTER 5

The phone rang agains as she sat thinking.
She hesitated to answer it when she saw that it was Megan on the line again. Still, she just couldn't resist picking up.

Hi Libs. It's me. I need a favor."

"What is it? I'm pretty busy here."

"Nothing too urgent. I just need you to pick up some groceries for me at the market. My in-laws are here as you know and I didn't get to the store yet. They won't have anything for dinner."

"Why can't you pick something up on your way home?"

"You know Laurel doesn't eat takeout. Besides, I have to work late tonight. By the time I get in it will be very late."

"And what about Ron? They're his parents," Libby pointed out.

"He was called out of town unexpectedly. It's just me and them at home for the next two days. You know how Laurel and I are. She tries everything she can think of to find fault.

She's upset that I haven't made her a grandmother yet. You know what she says…."

"'A woman isn't a woman unless she has children.' Yes, I remember," Libby groaned. She knew what was coming. She was going to have to skip lunch and leave early again in order to help her sister.

"Libs, please?"

"Alright, alright," she conceded huffily.

"Excellent! Thank you. Oh, could you possibly pick up my dry-cleaning from too? It's on your way. And if you could possibly make something quick for dinner I'd be eternally grateful. If Laurel has to cook there'll be no end of complaining…."

Libby was speechless. Her sister had gone from her collecting groceries, to picking up laundry and cooking for in-laws that weren't even her own!

"Megan, I'm working on a really big project right now. I'm up for a promotion."

"That's great. I'm sure you'll get it."

"But I really need to work on my presentation."

"You can still do that when you get home can't you? How long do you have?

"Just a few days."

"See, plenty of time to complete the task successfully. But today I really need you. Please, little sister?"

Libby sighed. She couldn't very well leave Megan in a bind. Her mother-in-law was the she-beast from hell.

If she didn't help now, she'd hear about it forever when Megan called to complain of the torment she was under.

"I'll leave work early, but you owe me," Libby replied tersely.

"I will treat you to dinner. Order anything you like."

"You owe me five dinners already."

"And you'll get them. As soon as I can, you'll get them." There was a pause. "Libs, I really have to go now. Do you have everything? Groceries, dry-cleaning, and dinner for my in-laws?"

"I have it, Megan."

"Great. Call you later."

The phone hung up immediately and Libby set the receiver down with a sigh. "No, you won't."

SHE GOT HOME AROUND NINE. The grocery store lines were longer than expected and it took a while to get to Megan's. Once there, she prepared the meal and chatted with her sister's in-laws. She'd stayed as long as she could to be polite, but Megan had yet to arrive by the time she left.

Libby strolled into the house and was met by a delighted Jingle. "Hey boy."

The little dog barked and began to circle, sniffing for any hidden treats.

"I didn't bring you anything, sorry. You're smelling the dinner I made for Megan," she said to him as she shuffled to the kitchen, kicking her heels off in the living room and walking barefoot.

When she passed the phone in the living room she was shocked to find there was a message. She pressed the button.

"Libs, you forgot the shirt I wanted to wear tomorrow –"

She stopped the message midway. Well, at least Megan had been honest.

She *did* call her later.

CHAPTER 6

The next day Libby found herself sitting on the couch in her living room looking over old photos.

Their father had been a constant photographer since before any of them were born. He had every traditional photo one could take during the holidays.

There were some of their mother putting the turkey in the oven. Some of Megan and Andy as children fighting over the last piece of stuffing. There was even a baby picture of Libby with fat cheeks and her face covered in chocolate frosting from the yule log.

"Such good times …" she said with a sad smile. She missed her parents. There were hardly any holiday photos since they had left them.

Libby had tried to step into her father's shoes but it was impossible when she was doing everything else. Still, she managed to take a few shots from time to time.

One year she had enlisted her eight-year-old nephew to do pictures and he'd taken plenty but there were far more out of focus than in.

Then she found a picture of her mother surrounded by all of her children. They were all grinning and her mom's cheeks were rosy and her smile bright.

"I miss you, Mom," Libby said softly. "This time of year just isn't the same without you and Dad. Things have changed and I don't know if you'd be happy about it. Andy and the others are hardly here anymore. It's almost Christmas and here I am again doing everything on my own. When you were around this would never have happened."

She chuckled lightly. "Do you remember? You and I would team up and tackle every task. The others would come to help once the smell of the food started to fill the house." She laughed sadly. "There's no one here now to do that though. I buy the groceries. Clean and decorate the house. Cook the food and clean it up after."

The phone rang. It always rang more often during the holidays.

"Hey big bro," Libby greeted, as she slid down in the couch and put her feet up on the arm of it.

Andy sounded as if he was driving. She could hear the sound of the traffic blowing past the window and sound of horns honking.

"I need to borrow your laptop if I could."

"What's the matter with yours?"

"It died this morning and I need it to finish a document for work tomorrow. Can I borrow yours?"

"OK, but you'll have it drop it back to me straight after. I need it for an important presentation that's in two days."

"I'll have it back. No worries."

"I mean it Andy. I need it back tomorrow so that I can finish the project in time. It might land me a promotion."

"It's about time you got one. You're the best they have."

"Thanks. It's for the Hershell Chocolate account."

"Hershell? That's a big deal. Are you sure you're ready?"

Her eyes widened. Didn't he just say she was the best they had? Libby did her best not to express her disappointment.

"Where are you?" she asked him.

"On my way to you."

"You mean you already knew that I'd let you borrow it?" she asked, a little taken aback.

"Sorry. But you never let us down, sis. It's something we can always be sure of."

CHAPTER 7

"Andy, it's me again. Why haven't you called me back? I need the laptop. Call me back."

Since she'd leant him the laptop Libby couldn't reach Andy on the phone.

She paced her office again, as nettles covered her skin.

The client would be here today and her stupid brother had done a disappearing act. Which she wouldn't have minded if it weren't for the fact that he still had her laptop!

Her phone rang minutes later and a wave of relief washed over her as she saw her brother's name appear on screen.

"Andy, where on earth are you? I've been calling and calling."

"I had to fly out to New York."

"*What?* New York, New York? But what about my laptop? I told you I needed it."

"I'm sorry. I had to take it with me, but I'm back now and I have it."

Libby's heart dropped into her stomach. "Oh my God. Where are you now?"

"At the airport. I just landed. I'm headed to you as soon as I get through arrivals."

Libby ran her fingers through her hair in dismay.

"The *airport*? Andy, that's too far. You won't get here in time. I told you I needed it back before the presentation!"

"I'm sorry. The work thing totally slipped my mind."

"The biggest day of my life and it slipped your mind?" Libby cried in disbelief.

She hung up. Her phone rang several times afterward but she wouldn't look at it.

Everything was ruined. Her PowerPoint was on that laptop and there was no way for her to access it otherwise. "I should have saved what I had to a memory stick ... why didn't I do that?" she winced, as tears filled her eyes.

The client would be arriving soon and she had nothing to show them.

Now, Libby walked toward Steven's office. She had to tell him the bad news. She had no idea how her boss would take it, but she was disappointed enough for both of them.

She passed Mark Clarke in the hall on the way there. There would be no end to his arrogance once he got the promotion. The entire marketing team would live to regret her foolishness.

Libby's pace slowed as she approached Steven's office. She looked at his nameplate outside, written in gold and trembled.

She couldn't believe this was happening. Her boss had given her a chance and now she was here to beg for another.

She took a deep breath, raised her hand and knocked.

"Come in."

Steven greeted her with a smile that Libby tried to return but failed.

Just as she'd failed at the task he'd given her.

"Libby, all ready for later?" he asked with a smile.

She hesitated. "Actually no. There was a problem with my laptop and I don't have the PowerPoint file to hand."

The words left her lips like molasses from a bottle on a cold day.

Steven's gaze leveled at her.

"What do you mean? Can't you just upload it to a PC here?"

She shook her head. She swallowed the lump in her throat.

"I didn't save and download it because it wasn't quite finished. Tomorrow - I can have it completed tomorrow. Is there any chance the client might be persuaded to delay until then?"

Libby was internally crossing her fingers and her toes.

She just needed another chance. She could have everything ready by tomorrow. She just needed time.

"There is nothing I can do for you, Libby. The client's only free window was today. Plus the board wants to make the announcement as soon as possible regarding the new senior marketing executive." Steven stood and walked toward her. He laid a comforting hand on her arm. "I'm sorry."

That was it. One mistake and she'd lost the biggest opportunity of her life.

She should never have allowed her brother to borrow her laptop. It was the company's, so she really should've known better anyway, but he needed her help.

Now she was paying for it.

"Steven," she pleaded. "Isn't there any way? I know this is really good."

"I'm sorry Libby. This was a one-time chance."

She stood dumbfounded as Steven turned his back on her and walked back to his seat. He sat with both hands on the armrests and looked at her. "If Mark successfully completes the presentation, I will announce his appointment at the Christmas party."

Libby stared at him for several seconds as she tried to internalize what he'd said.

She'd blown it. It was over. Really and truly over.

"Thank you for the opportunity. I'm so sorry I let you down," Libby said softly as she lowered her eyes in shame.

"Not more than me. I was sure you were the best person for this position, but I had to prove it to the board," Steven said bitterly. "It'll be a hard pill to swallow when I have to go back to them."

"Steven, just twenty-four hours?" Libby pleaded again. "That's all I need. I know my presentation will blow them away. I'm sure of it. If you could just postpone it for a day? A few hours, even. I can get it all together for you. I can make this happen."

"I wish I could, Libby. I really wish I could. But there is nothing I can do. Hershells set the timing because it worked with their schedule. There is no tomorrow or a few hours. It's now or never."

CHAPTER 8

Libby could barely process anything as she trudged slowly back to her office.

People passed her on the way to wish her good luck with the presentation, but nothing reached her.

She returned to her office, closed and locked the door and then sat at her desk and wept.

Her eyes were puffy and sore by the time someone knocking on her door got her attention.

She forced herself to wipe her face and got a tissue to blow her nose before she dared open it.

Unlocking the door, she took a deep breath. Sharon was standing there with the saddest look on her face.

"I heard."

Libby let her in and then quickly closed the door behind her. People in the hall were staring. She couldn't deal with them right now.

"What happened?" her friend asked.

Libby walked around her desk and flopped into her chair.

"You had this. What went wrong?" Sharon persisted.

"Me. That's what went wrong. Me."

"You? What did you do?"

"I loaned my brother the laptop when he had an emergency with work. I told him I needed it back the next day. He forgot and took it with him to New York."

Sharon's eyes looked as if they were about to explode from her skull. "Are … you … *kidding* me?" she bellowed

"Shhh…keep your voice down."

"How can *you* keep your voice down? Your brother shafts you over the biggest opportunity of your life, and you're this calm about it?"

"It was my fault. I should never have lent it to him in the first place. It was company property, not mine. I was the idiot here."

"Libby, are you for real? You're blaming yourself for this? Your brother is the absolute worst! Yes, you were wrong to give him the laptop, but he was worse for not bringing it back when he knew you needed it. He really took it to New York?" Sharon's head was shaking as she sighed deeply.

"It doesn't matter now," Libby stated. "It's over."

"Libby, for goodness sake, get angry. Do something. This can't go on. You can't spend the rest of your life being your siblings' scapegoat for everything. You need to think of having a life of your own. I know you want to hold on to traditions, but for your own sake, you need to create new ones."

Sharon was on her feet a moment later and striding to the door. "Think about it. Someone has to give."

Leaving Libby alone and confused.

She thought about everything that had happened over the last few days and weeks - the endless demands and requests for 'favors'.

And Andy's words as he casually drove to borrow the laptop he already knew she'd lend him.

You never let us down, sis. It's something we can always be sure of.

CHAPTER 9

The following afternoon, Libby dropped her stuff at her front door, stomped into the living room and flopped down on the couch with a groan.

Andrew had since apologised about the incident with the laptop by saying there would be other promotions and not to sweat the small stuff. Small stuff. He saw the biggest opportunity of her career as 'small stuff.'!

It was getting beyond ridiculous.

Today she'd received another call from Eden informing her that *her* in-laws had come in early to surprise them, and could Libby take her children and their friends Christmas shopping?

She'd spent three hours with eight children between the ages of six and ten, as she tried to help them manage their money and pick up the toys they were searching for.

It was a test of anyone's nerves and Libby's were well and truly fried.

Jingle trotted into the room and flopped on the rug by her feet. "Hey little guy," she said with a frustrated sigh. He looked at her with his big dark eyes and snorted. "That's exactly how I feel," she replied as she stretched out a hand to scratch behind his ears.

She lay on the couch for several minutes as she decided whether she wanted to move or not. Her feet hurt, her back hurt and she was hungry. She had taken the children shopping but she wasn't about to manage all of them at one table with food too.

She rolled onto her side and noticed the light blinking on the phone. Another message from Andy. Maybe he'd had second thoughts and was calling to properly apologise?

"Hi, Libs. Meet me at the mall tomorrow? I need some help finding a present for Molly. I'll be there around five. Meet you at the west entrance. Bye!"

She couldn't speak. Tears were stinging the backs of her eyes.

"He didn't even ask," she said to herself as a tear rolled down her cheek. *None* of them ever asked, or if they did, they took it for granted that the answer would be yes and if it wasn't they made a fuss until it was.

"OK, that's *it*," she announced, so loud that it made Jingle jump up from his nap. The dog gave a started yelp as he tried to figure out what was going on. "Enough."

She got to her feet and hurried upstairs, Jingle scurrying after her.

"Someplace warm," she muttered to herself as she began rummaging in her closet. She pulled out her suitcase and tossed it on the bed.

Libby wasn't thinking, she was just packing. She found her bathing suit, some shorts, a few dresses, and shoes. Anything that would work.

"If they think I'm sticking around to be their Christmas

Girl Friday this year, they're mistaken," she said angrily. Jingle was completely bewildered and stuck his nose in her stuff to see what was going on.

When the suitcase was packed she opened her laptop and began searching for flights. Her favorite discount site had tons of offers but nothing was grabbing her.

That is until she saw a special and her eyes widened. *Hawaii?*

Perfect.

Libby didn't hesitate; she booked the flight and used her discount coupon to get a further $25 off her ticket.

"Now where to stay…" she asked as she began another search. Jingle barked beside her. "I know. You're hungry," she commented as her fingers nimbly skated over the keys. Her eyes flicked through pictures of potential accommodation, but it was taking longer than expected and Jingle was getting increasingly agitated.

While Libby was starting to feel increasingly better, as the prospect of a quieter, more relaxing Christmas materialized.

She hummed a festive tune as she danced around the kitchen pulling together something for herself for dinner. She grabbed kibble from the cupboard and a can of canned dog food. She mixed them together and put them in Jingle's bowl. He was already eating before she got it to the floor, and so she returned to her laptop.

There were so many options to choose from, but she didn't want to stay anywhere too commercial or crazy.

So the Marriott and the like were definitely out.

Then Libby came across an option for a guesthouse just a few minutes drive from the airport, and right on the beach.

"Kalea Inn," she mused out loud, as she began to skim the reviews. They were all overwhelmingly positive. The place rated four and a half stars which was excellent, and the price was perfect.

Finally, her decision was made. She pressed the 'Book' button and it was done.

Libby smiled to herself as she leaned against the kitchen counter.

This year, she was getting out of town and heading for somewhere a million miles from small town Christmas central.

She needed an escape.

CHAPTER 10

Four days later Libby was standing outside Kona Airport waiting for her ride.

The guesthouse owner had sent her an email about her booking at the Kalea Inn later that same night and they'd been corresponding over the past few days to ensure that everything was ready for her arrival.

The second she stepped off the plane Libby found herself with a beautiful purple lei around her neck and she smiled.

Outside, the sun was blissfully bright and warm, and the air tropical. It was just what she was hoping for.

A warm breeze blew across her face as she waited for someone from the inn to pick her up. She got her phone out and called home.

"Hey Sharon how's Jingle?"

Her friend was dog-sitting for the week she'd be gone.

Before leaving she'd called Andy to let him and the others know she was going away and wasn't going to be back until after Christmas.

That didn't go over well but Libby hadn't listened long enough to hear his surprise or remonstration.

She'd made up her mind and she wasn't letting anyone change it.

A jeep pulled up and a man got out.

The vehicle was like something she'd seen on safari videos on Discovery Channel, but the side of it read Kalea Inn.

Libby's eyes grew large at the sight of the man walking toward her. He was over six feet tall and the roots of his hair were dark but the ends were lighter from the sun.

His skin was golden tan and his short-sleeved cotton shirt clung to his muscles. On his left arm, the ends of a black tattoo peeked out from beneath the sleeve. His chin was covered in a short, neatly cropped beard beneath a mustache.

The guy should be on the cover of a romance novel.

The man strode toward her, a folded sign in his hands which he opened as he looked around.

It took Libby a few seconds to notice the name on the card was her own.

She walked toward him and dragged her bag behind her.

"I'm Libby," she said brightly as she flashed him a smile. He looked at her and gave a polite smile so quick that if she blinked she would've missed it.

"Rob," he nodded. "Welcome to Kohala."

"Thanks. Nice to meet you. It's good to have a face to go with the name," she replied amiably. She was smiling more than she should but she couldn't help it. She was in a tropical paradise for the holidays, and her driver looked like someone from a movie.

"Sure," he replied as he took Libby's luggage and started for the jeep.

She looked around as she followed him. "Isn't there anyone else?"

"You're it today," Rob said as he hoisted her bag into the back. "You can sit up front with me," he added as he walked to the driver's side and got in.

Libby walked around the front of the vehicle. He opened the door for her from the inside and she climbed in.

The cabin of the car was neat. She couldn't help the surreptitious inspection as she got in. His car was much cleaner than hers. She always had an extra pair of shoes or three on the passenger side.

Rob started the engine and they began the journey to the inn. Lava fields spread before her in red and black earth splendor, amidst verdant palm trees.

Libby could hardly believe she was really in Hawaii.

"It's so beautiful," she commented to herself as she stared out at the landscape.

"You said it was your first time to the island?" Rob questioned. He was driving with one hand and leaning on the window with the other.

"Very first," Libby answered. "And you? You've been here long?"

"Seven years," he answered shortly.

"I guess this beauty is normal to you, then."

Rob didn't answer. He just looked out the window.

"So how far is it?" she asked eventually.

"Just over twenty minutes. The inn is just up past Waialea Beach."

Libby smiled at the way the strange names rolled off his tongue. He looked like he belonged on an ad for lumberjacks or something. She could definitely see him in one of her ad campaigns. He'd be perfect.

"What?" he asked shortly. She was so lost in her own head she hadn't realized she was staring.

"Sorry," she laughed. "I was just thinking."

"Your mother never teach you that you don't stare?"

Now Libby was a bit taken back by his abruptness. "Actually she did. Sorry," she replied shortly.

So much for an Aloha welcome.

The drive took less time than she imagined. Twenty minutes went by very quickly when everything around was so spectacular.

The next thing Libby knew they were stopped outside a simple two-storey building, painted in cream with a brown roof and trim.

What stood out to her was that there wasn't a single Christmas decoration apparent. She glanced around a little more while Rob unloaded her bag.

Nope, nothing.

"You guys don't decorate for the holidays?" she asked in surprise. The rest of the Big Island she'd seen on the way had some signs of festive cheer, but not the Kalea Inn.

"I don't do Christmas," Rob answered gruffly. "This way to check-in."

Libby's forehead wrinkled as she followed him into the building.

What did he mean that he didn't *do* Christmas? Who didn't do Christmas?

But there wasn't a smile on his face and she knew instinctively that he wasn't joking.

They were met at reception by a pretty dark-haired woman who had a brilliant smile.

"Apikalia, could you see that Ms. Pearson gets checked in. She's in room nine," Rob informed her as he left Libby's bag at the desk and then disappeared into a room behind it.

"Mele Kalikimaka," the receptionist said brightly. "Welcome to the Kalea Inn."

Libby swallowed, realising that if she truly wanted to escape Christmas, she'd very definitely picked the right place.

CHAPTER 11

❄

The next couple of days passed by in a blur and Libby was loving every second of it. She'd *definitely* made the right choice to embark on a last minute adventure.

Her room was on the top floor overlooking the ocean. The guesthouse had its own private beach, a secluded cove up the coast from Waialea.

In fact, there was nothing else nearby as far as the eye could see; the absolute perfect getaway.

It was also nice to have people taking care of her instead of the other way round. Libby usually didn't mind, but after a while, it began to weigh on you, especially when the people you were doing it for didn't seem to care just how much it was taking out of you.

Today she wore a red sundress with a white tropical flower print along the skirt. It was sleeveless and showed off her slightly toned arms.

She'd worked very hard for that little bit of tone. Libby tended to be softer; she wasn't overweight, but she had gentle curves and a propensity to gain even more of those if she didn't pay attention.

Mint green sandals were on her feet. She had a matching bag too, but she didn't have plans to leave the inn that day. She just wanted to spend it on the beach enjoying the warm breezes and golden sunshine.

She walked down to the breakfast area and found it relatively full, but there were still a few tables available.

The inn had twelve rooms and they were all occupied for the festive season.

Libby had briefly encountered several of her fellow guests over the past few days, but none touched her heart like Naomi - a seventy-three-year-old woman who reminded her so much of her mother.

Now she walked over to where the older woman was sitting. "Good morning."

"Nice to see you, dear. Join me?"

Libby didn't need to be asked twice. She pulled out the chair beside Naomi and took a seat. "Thanks for letting me sit with you. How're you doing today?"

"I'm very well thank you. How are you?"

"Great. Have you ordered already?" She skimmed over the menu. There weren't many choices, but what they had was fresh and always wonderful.

"I was just waiting for the waitress," Naomi informed her. "What are your plans today?"

"Nothing," Libby sighed happily. "Just enjoying the sunshine. What about you?" she asked as the waitress poured water when they'd placed their orders.

"Well, I'm on a mission today actually," the older woman said intriguingly. She then turned to the vacant seat beside her and picked up a silver urn.

"I'm going to see my Charlie off," she added with a gentle smile.

"Oh Naomi ..." Libby began but she wasn't sure what she wanted to say.

The older woman had mentioned her husband had died but she didn't realize it was so recently.

Naomi smiled as she patted the top of the urn lovingly. "He always wanted to come back here," she said. "He proposed to me on this island fifty years ago. We planned to come back this Christmas to commemorate it, but poor Charlie didn't make it."

Libby swallowed the lump that had formed in her throat. She couldn't help it, hearing Naomi's heartbreaking words made her want to cry.

"Don't get upset," the other woman said brightly. "Charlie wouldn't want anyone crying over him. He always lived his life a second at a time, and he enjoyed every minute of it. That's why I'm here. He wanted me to come, even though he wasn't going to be with me in body, but promised he'd be with me in spirit." Naomi hugged the urn to her before setting it back on its seat.

"Where on the island are you going?" Libby asked as the waitress returned with their coffee and juice.

"To Pu'u Ku'ili," she replied, referring to the famed old cinder cone, a popular sightseeing spot on the island.

"How are you getting there?"

"I've arranged a ride," the woman answered.

Libby looked aghast. "You're going to do this alone?"

"It's fine. I promised Charlie. The sooner the better to get it over with."

Libby was resolute. There was no way she was going to allow that. "If you don't mind the company ...may I come with you?"

A small smile spread across Naomi's face. "Are you sure?"

"I'd really love it if you'd allow me," Libby replied. "I'd feel a whole lot better knowing you weren't alone."

"I'd like that."

The pair continued to sit and talk while they waited for breakfast to arrive. Once it did they took turns sampling from the other's choice and laughing about having made the wrong decision for themselves.

It felt good to just enjoy a meal with someone and actually make plans with them, instead of hearing their demands.

Libby truly wanted to be there for Naomi. She couldn't imagine saying goodbye forever to the one you loved would be easy.

She'd never been married, not even close, but she remembered the interactions of her parents. Theirs was the ideal that she based all her relationships on.

Her parents had a love that transcended most norms. They genuinely loved one another and sacrificed for the other.

It seemed Naomi and Charlie's marriage had been the same.

CHAPTER 12

After breakfast, Libby excused herself momentarily to get her bag from her room and rushed back, unwilling to keep Naomi waiting long.

On the way, she ran into Rob – literally. Their shoulders collided as she was going up the stairs and he was coming down.

"Sorry," she apologized in a rush as she continued on her journey up. She felt his questioning gaze follow her but she didn't turn around.

Minutes later she was rushing through the reception area outside to where she'd told Naomi she'd meet her.

The older woman was already standing beside the inn's jeep.

"All set?" Libby asked.

"We were waiting for you," Naomi replied.

"We?"

A second later Rob stepped out from the other side of the jeep. He looked at her silently and Libby felt the hairs on the back of her neck stand on end.

He had an intense expression on his face that even though not unpleasant, formed knots in her stomach.

"Rob said he'd take us," Naomi informed her.

"Let's get you ladies boarded so we can get going," he stated as he stepped forward to help Naomi into the jeep. He turned to Libby after and gave her a hand into the back.

She sat on the bench that lined the back of the jeep's flatbed and watched as the lava fields once again came into view.

Once or twice she thought she caught Rob's eyes looking back at her in the rearview mirror. It was nice of him to offer to take Naomi here today.

And a little perplexing how he could be so cold one minute, then do something kind and courteous the next.

It wasn't long before they arrived at Pu'u Ku'ili.

Rob drove them as far as he could along the trail, but they still had to walk a short distance to get to the top.

He held Naomi's hand while Libby carried the urn.

When they reached the summit Libby stood on the cone and looked around her.

The view was unforgettable. Inland, the earth was charred and the dirt either black or a dark red. There was hardly any vegetation nearby, but in the distance, she could see sprigs of grass and the green of a few shrubs.

Towards the ocean, she could see buildings standing uniformly together, their roofs various shades of brown and more greenery to be found nearby. The ocean was the most beautiful blue she'd ever seen. Paler near the shore, it deepened from azure to a rich cerulean.

It was breath-taking.

"Give Charlie to me," Naomi asked then, as Libby stood staring. She nodded quickly and handed the urn over.

Then she stepped back a little to where Rob stood a few feet away, to allow Naomi the privacy needed for her last farewell to her husband.

Libby watched as it unfolded. She wanted to make sure Naomi was all right, but she also couldn't help but admire how unaffected and unflinching she was to so something she herself was sure would have her in tears.

She wondered where the woman got the strength from.

"It must be such a horrible thing to lose the one you love," she mumbled to Rob as they watched. "To have to say goodbye after so many wonderful years together. Knowing that you will never see them again."

He exhaled. "Hurts no matter how long you were together," he muttered, much to her surprise.

Libby turned to face him but found he wasn't looking at her at all, but at Naomi.

Her gaze shifted to where the older woman stood. Was that it? The reason he always seemed so cagey and distant? Had he lost someone too?

She turned back to Rob and this time their eyes met. "Why did you come?" he asked. "You don't even know her."

"You don't have to know someone well to want to be there for them through something difficult," she answered, then turned back to Naomi. "I just didn't want to let her do this alone."

"Neither did I," he said and Libby's eyes moved back to him. "Like you said, it isn't something you should do alone, especially at her age."

Maybe he wasn't as boorish as she'd first believed him to be. Maybe he was just a man who was dealing with something she could never understand. Something that Naomi could though.

Did Rob truly identify with the older woman's loss? Was that why he couldn't let her say goodbye alone?

Libby had more questions now than when she'd first met him. Who exactly was Rob and why was he in Kohala?

He obviously wasn't a native Hawaiian. So what had brought him to the islands to run the inn?

The faint sound of a song wafted toward Libby's ears then and both she and Rob again focused their attention back on Naomi. She was singing.

It was an old song, something from the forties or fifties Libby guessed. She was swaying in place as she turned the urn over and allowed her late husband's ashes to spill into the breeze to every note.

"Goodbye Charlie …" Libby whispered to herself as she watched the scene.

Now the older woman walked toward them, the empty urn hugged to her chest. She smiled. "He's gone now," she said. "He'd be happy."

Libby couldn't help it; she had to give Naomi a hug. The older woman accepted her embrace and patted her back soothingly. "Thank you for being here - both of you," she said.

"You're welcome," Rob answered quietly. "It was an honor."

CHAPTER 13

Later, Libby couldn't sleep, still affected by the events of the day. She kept thinking of her family and wondering how they were doing.

Her siblings had been calling her incessantly since her arrival, and while she was happy to send the odd text, she still refused to take any calls.

This trip was all about escape, some time for herself, away from them.

She stood on the balcony outside her room and looked out over the dark water. The sky and sea seemed to meet like ink on the horizon. Only the stars differentiated one from the other.

She leaned against the rail, the silk nightgown she wore danced around her calves as she watched the white peaks of waves appear and disappear in the distance.

Half an hour passed and she was still unable to sleep. So she changed into a sundress and went downstairs for a walk.

Voices coming from the dining room caught her attention as she headed for the front door.

She followed the sound to find Rob and two other men sitting talking around a small table.

"Seems we aren't the only night owls," the first man commented when he saw her in the doorway. She recognised him as another guest.

He was cleanly shaven with a bald head and a slender face.

"I'm sorry. I didn't mean to intrude. I just heard voices …" Libby explained hesitantly.

"No intrusion. Come on in," the man said with a friendly wave of his hand beckoning her to join them.

Another man sat beside him. He looked similar, though his hair was dark and closely cropped, and his face fuller and more tanned.

"I'm Nate," the other guest said as he extended her hand to her. "This is my twin brother Greg."

Now Libby saw the resemblance. It was in the eyes. They both had bright blue eyes.

"Libby," she answered as she shook each man's hand in turn. She looked at their host. "Rob."

He nodded but said nothing. He was reclined in his seat with his foot folded over the other casually and his arms crossed over his stomach.

"So what brings you to the island?" Greg asked with a smile.

She smiled. "Escaping Christmas," she admitted truthfully. "Family mostly."

"They giving you a hard time?"

"More like they don't see me as anything more than their go-fetch-it girl," she chuckled but there was no mirth to it. "My favorite time of the year, and all I hear from them is what they need from me. No one ever seems to realize that I need things too."

"Material stuff you mean?" Nate questioned.

"No. More for them to be there for me the way I'm always there for them. It gets pretty tiring being the one whom everyone depends on, yet there is no one there when you need the same."

"Well, my poor brother knows all about that," Nate laughed and Libby looked at him and Greg curiously. "I have cancer," he blurted out then and she was taken completely by surprise.

She fumbled for something to say and found herself tongue-tied.

"You don't have to say anything. You were on the subject of dependency and I just wanted to make things clear from the start," Nate continued.

"I'm so sorry," she muttered.

"I told you that you didn't have to say anything," he smiled. "People always say they're sorry. It's nice but unnecessary. I'm alright. I've made peace with everything."

"So Kohala is part of your adventure?" Libby asked.

"It's the seventh thing on my bucket list."

Libby was completely astounded at Nate's positivity. She had never met anyone who knew they were dying.

She couldn't imagine what that must feel like to know that your end was imminent. The thought gave her a slight chill.

"Rob was telling us that you helped Naomi scatter her husband's ashes the other day," Nate continued while his brother sat quietly and Libby could immediately see that while he had accepted his fate, Greg had not.

They chatted on for a while before eventually Nate yawned. "I think it's time for me to go. I'm getting tired."

"Goodnight guys," Greg said as he helped his brother to his feet.

"Goodnight to you both," Libby replied. "See you guys in the morning."

"Maybe we can do breakfast?" Nate suggested. "I'd love to hear more about your work for the chocolate company."

"See you here."

Libby watched the brothers as they went.

It was odd, but meeting them only made her think of her own family even more. Nate and Greg depended on each other and there was no animosity between them. One was dying and the other was doing everything he could to be there for him.

It made her feel like her problems with her siblings were silly really.

Now, she turned to look at Rob. He'd remained quiet for most of the conversation, only choosing to say something if a question was directed to him.

She shifted uncomfortably in her seat. Maybe she should go now too? It wasn't as if Rob was going to stay on and chat. He hardly ever spoke to her.

"How's Naomi?" he asked then.

"Great. I had dinner with her earlier."

"Good," Rob replied. "The other day must've brought up a lot of memories. Good and bad."

Libby watched him carefully. The visit to Pu'u Ku'ili had affected more than just Naomi.

"Who did you lose?" she asked softly. She watched him as she spoke and his face was impassive as he turned to her.

"What makes you think I lost someone?"

She smiled weakly. "I recognize it. When I lost my parents I looked like that whenever someone started talking about them," Libby explained.

Rob stared at her for a long time and she could see the hesitation in his eyes. "My wife."

"Your wife? I'm ... so sorry."

"Her name was Kalea. I named this place after her. She was born on the island and wanted to come back to start a business and give back to the community. We poured everything we had into getting this place. Then she died, so I was left to run it alone."

Libby couldn't imagine how he felt losing his wife. "I truly am sorry Rob. May I ask what happened to her?"

"A brain tumor. We were married for just over a year when it got her," he continued. "On Christmas Eve."

Which explained why there were no decorations and why Rob didn't do Christmas. He was still missing his wife.

"She loved this time of year. It was what she lived for really. The holidays and decorations, and family get togethers. Kalea always wanted to make people happy."

Libby felt a tear roll down her cheek as Rob talked about his late wife. There was still so much love in his voice.

"I'm sorry. This is hard for you. I shouldn't have asked," Libby apologised as she wiped her cheek.

"I don't know why I'm telling you actually," he continued. "I never talk about her to anyone. It must be everything with Naomi ... and now Nate that has me thinking about her." He turned to her. "Sorry for getting you down."

"Don't apologize. I asked."

"When did you lose your parents?" He had turned in his seat to face her better. It was the first time Libby noticed how bright his eyes were, even in sadness.

"Six years ago. They died days apart, and it was pretty much left to me to take over everything they cared about," she admitted. "All our family's stuff. The house. Traditions. It all became my responsibility."

"Why you? Didn't you say you had siblings?"

"Four of them," Libby answered. "They all have families of their own. Children and in-laws. They don't have much time for anything else."

"Including you, I take it?"

Her cheeks warmed at the inquiry. "Sometimes I feel like I'm a servant instead of their sister. Running around to pick up their children. Collect their dry-cleaning and deal with upholding our family stuff all on my own. It's been hard. Honestly, this year I was so tired of having to do everything for the holidays that I decided that I wasn't - going to do it, I mean. That's why I came here."

"Do you hate them?"

Her eyes grew wide. "No. Of course not. I love them a lot. That's why it hurts so much to be treated like I don't matter to them. That what's important to me, means nothing to them at all."

"I understand," Rob said as he got to his feet. "It isn't easy to bear the weight of a legacy on your shoulders. Or someone else dream."

Libby stood too, feeling tired all of a sudden, and realising that she and Rob kind of understood each other in some strange way.

He was doing all of this in the name of a wife who could no longer fulfil her dream, while she was doing all she could to keep her parent's traditions alive.

"Walk you back to your room?" he stated as he started for the door.

"How do you do it?" she asked, following as he left the dining room and up the stairs.

"Do what?"

"Continue on every day on your own with no one here who understands?"

"I surf," Rob said with a smile. "When I'm out on the waves there isn't anything for me to worry about. It's just me and the waves. It makes me think of her. She loved the water. We met at a surf competition in California. It was love on the waves," he said with a smile. "I knew the first time I saw her cruise through that curl that I'd found the perfect woman for me."

Libby smiled. "It sounds wonderful."

"It was wonderful." He looked around him. "I know she would've done more with this place, especially now, but I just can't seem to get my mind there."

"I'll be honest with you. I was wondering about it when I arrived. I was surprised that there were no Christmas decorations, or anything remotely festive."

He sighed. "I don't know why I should bother really. No one's complaining. Except for you," he added lightly.

Libby considered what he'd said as they walked the corridor to her room.

There were quite a few people here escaping the holidays for their own, mostly sad reasons. Even the owner had a tale of woe.

Maybe, despite what Rob thought, Kalea Inn *did* need a dash of Christmas spirit to brighten the mood and hearts of everyone staying there.

CHAPTER 14

❄

Slowly but surely, Libby was falling in love with Hawaii.

She was used to the fast pace of the marketing world, but here, they did things differently.

It was the most relaxed Christmas she'd ever had. No running to the grocery store a thousand times to stand in mile-long lines. No excessive list of gifts to buy, because Christmas wasn't Christmas if you didn't break your credit card with buying toys and presents.

Then there was the absurd pressure she put on herself to make sure everything was just as her mother and father would have made it when they were alive. They way her siblings expected it.

No, life didn't have to be that way.

Today, the sand was cool as she walked along the beach in her brand new swimsuit. She was still a bit bashful so she'd bought a cute floral print, halter neck tankini her second day on the island. It fit her perfectly and made her feel confident about her body without making her feel exposed.

The wind skated off the ocean sending a cool breeze over her skin. Libby couldn't help but smile at how wonderful it was to feel sand between her toes and smell the salty freshness of the ocean.

She looked out onto the water. Whitecaps peaked the waves, and a lone surfer occupied the water beyond the reef. She stopped to watch.

The waters near the inn weren't the type that called international surfers to try their luck, these were calm and could easily be manoeuvred by a novice.

Beyond the reef, however, the waves were larger, forming into curls, and the surfer was making the most of them. Lowering beneath the barrelling edge of a wave he was a master on the board.

Libby never pretended to be brave. Climbing on a surfboard and going out into water she couldn't stand in and probably couldn't even *swim* in, was not her cup of tea.

However, it didn't mean she didn't appreciate watching those who could. She stood and watched as the surfer tamed the waves and rode the final one into shore not far from where she stood. She stared as he carried his board in, dragging his long dark hair back with a hand before jogging in her direction.

It was only as he got closer that she realized who it was.

Rob nodded at her. "I see you're out early," he commented.

"It's such a beautiful day I thought a walk on the beach would do me good," she answered.

"Just on the beach? The water's perfect."

Libby looked at the ocean. He was right, it did look inviting. "I haven't done much swimming since I got here ..."

"How much have you done?"

"None actually," she laughed. "I've been spending my days

wandering or sunbathing or just meeting people. I've met so many nice people since I arrived here. You wouldn't believe some of the stories I've heard."

"I can imagine actually," Rob informed her lightly. "You'd be surprised how many broken-hearted and lonely people end up here."

Libby thought about what he was saying. She'd already encountered a number of people with stories like those of Naomi, Nate, and Greg.

Even a few like her who felt unappreciated and were seeking a change.

However, she also saw another element. She saw what they were truly after – a getaway from Christmas commercialism to somewhere more laidback and easygoing, where they could find their own kind of peace and joy away from the noise of traditional festivity.

"Rob, have you ever thought of doing something different for Christmas?" Libby asked then.

His forehead wrinkled. "Like what?"

"Not traditional stuff obviously, but different to what other places offer at this time of year. I'm talking about something beyond the surface. Something that touches the heart."

"I never really thought about it," he admitted as he studied her carefully.

"Well, I have."

Libby took a deep breath. What she was about to suggest was insane and completely none of her business, but it was something that had been nagging her since the other night.

"I work in marketing for a living. I'm used to figuring out what people want and giving it to them. It's how you sell. You give people what they want, or make them *believe* they want something they never even knew they did."

"You think this place needs better marketing?" Rob questioned with some skepticism.

"Not marketing per se. I'm talking about doing something for the people here who are trying to get back to what Christmas is truly about."

The moment the words left her mouth Rob's expression changed. The lines in his forehead smoothed out and he sort of squinted at her.

Then he laughed softly. "That sounds like something Kalea would've said."

Libby wasn't sure if resembling something his late wife would've thought of was good or bad, but it didn't stop her from presenting her case.

"Your wife wanted this place to mean something. You said so yourself. It was her dream. So this year, why don't you make it the dream of all the staff and guests too?"

Rob stuck his board in the sand. "What exactly do you have in mind?"

She smiled. "A day of honoring what Christmas is really all about. No gifts, or spending money on each other; just sharing time together instead."

Rob's small laugh grew to a chuckle as she continued. "You sound more and more like her the more I listen to you."

"Then your wife was a very wise woman," Libby grinned.

Rob's eyes met hers. "She was."

She felt her stomach knot as he looked at her.

"Do you surf?" he asked unexpectedly.

"No," Libby laughed. "I've never even tried."

"I can teach you."

She shook her head. "I don't know about that..."

"I'll make you a deal," he countered. "If you let me teach

you the basics about surfing, I'll allow you to execute this ... plan of yours."

Libby's eyes grew wide. Did he just say he'd let her run with her idea? She couldn't describe the feeling in her stomach. It was like getting another shot at the promotion she'd missed out on.

"Great. So where do we start?"

"First things first," Rob chuckled. "Hold your board with two hands when you're carrying it out. You can tuck it under your arm like this when you're on the beach," he said as he showed her what to do, then handed the board to her for her to try.

Libby tucked the board under her arm.

"This is going to be too long for you given your height and weight," he informed. "You'd need one more than a foot shorter. But I can still show you a few things with it before we hit the water"

Libby nodded until she realized. "Hit the water?"

"Yes," Rob smiled. "You can't surf if you aren't comfortable out there," he said as he turned toward the water. "I need to see how you handle yourself."

Seems she was going to get wet that morning after all.

CHAPTER 15

❄

Rob continued to explain the basics of surfing while Libby listened quietly, nodding and following his example when she needed to.

Before she knew it, he was telling her it was time to hit the water. She waded out into the surf as he led the way.

Her heart was beating a bit faster in her chest as the sea climbed higher and higher up along her body.

She was good for a few feet but soon she could no longer feel the bottom and had to begin to tread water.

"You okay?" he asked as he looked back at her. He looked so at home in the ocean. His limbs moved effortlessly to keep him up.

Libby felt like a failed experiment. It had been so long it felt unnatural. Still, she vaguely remembered what to do.

"Yes. I'm fine," she replied.

He smiled at her and held out his hand. "Take my hand."

Libby didn't think twice about the offer. A second later he'd pulled her to him and they were face-to-face.

"You sure you're okay?"

"Yes," she said a little breathlessly. "I just haven't been swimming in a long time. I just need to get back in the swing of things."

"Don't be scared," he said firmly, but comfortingly. "I've got you."

She nodded as he led her closer to the reef. She wasn't sure how deep the water was, but she knew it was a lot darker beneath than it had been before.

"Do you think you can hold your breath?" Rob asked.

"Why?" she asked with just a pinch of fear.

"There's something I'd like to show you, but you have to go underwater to see it," he said as the waves lapped around his shoulders. He once again raked a hand through his hair to remove it from his face.

"Okay. Show me."

"Hold your breath."

Libby did as she was told, and the next second she was descending beneath the waves. She blinked several times to adjust her eyes to the salt. The moment they did so, the most spectacular sight greeted her.

Waving fans and corals of multiple colors stretched out before her. There were some that looked like fingers and others that looked like spines. More looked like purple flower clusters.

A turtle swam by and Rob turned to point it out as it approached. Above the water it was amazing but below, it was … incredible. The turtle was at least three feet long with a head and fins covered in dark scales.

Libby breathed deeply as her head broke the surface. Rob was still beneath. He was better at holding his breath than she was.

The waves were rolling in faster now. The tide seemed to be coming in.

"What did you think?" he asked when they'd both resurfaced.

"It was spectacular."

"Maybe I can take you snorkeling some time and we can see more of it," he suggested.

"I'd love that. But right now," she said as her head bobbed above another wave. "I think we should go back. The tide's getting a little higher."

Rob seemed completely unaffected, but Libby was getting nervous.

They swam back side-by-side and sat on the shore after, enjoying the sun. It warmed her skin and Libby couldn't remember having a better time in her life.

Rob turned to her. "So what do you need me to do for this Christmas plan of yours?" he asked.

Libby smiled. "Not much. I think I've got this covered."

CHAPTER 16

❄

It was quite shocking to Libby how many people were just skating through the holidays, hoping to stay above water.

Some wanted to forget. Some needed money. Others, like her, just wanted to escape Christmas.

The more people she talked to, the more Libby realized the idea was a lot bigger than she imagined.

One example was Tua, one of the waiters from the dining room. He had no family and saw the holidays as a time to distract himself from the fact that he was alone.

Ululani, one of the girls who cleaned the rooms, had a family that had fallen on hard times. Her mother and father were both out of work and she had six younger siblings to take care of. She was nineteen and the sole breadwinner. She was working because if she didn't they'd have nothing to even remotely resemble the Christmases they once enjoyed.

Though Libby wasn't just learning the bad, but the good too.

"Every year my mother would make these amazing

coconut biscuits," Ululani said with a smile. "They were like dog biscuits almost, really hard with a good crack and so much flavor. We'd help her roll them out, cut them up and then bake them."

"What about this year?" Libby questioned.

Ulalani shook her head. "Not this year."

"Why not?' she asked. "You can still hold on to the good despite everything."

"Tell that to my mother," Ululani answered. "Since she and dad lost their jobs they've sort of lost themselves as well. They worry and they try to find work. That's all they do. Now it's Christmas and nothing is the same. This is the third holiday since it happened. The first year they tried, believing that work would come. The second, things weren't so great. This year is horrible. If it weren't for Rob letting me work here, I don't know what we'd do."

"He seems like a really good guy," Libby stated.

"The best," Ululani said as she turned the sheet over at the top and tucked it beneath the mattress. "It's a shame he's always alone."

"What do you mean?"

"You know. He doesn't have anyone. You'd think someone like him would be drowning in women, but he barely even notices them," the young woman divulged.

"Seriously?"

"Yeah. I guess he still misses his wife."

"Did you know her?"

"No. She died before I found out about this place, but Honi who works in maintenance, he was here from the very beginning. He said she was a really great woman. Kind, like Rob and that everyone was really sorry when she died." She sighed.

"They said if he hadn't had this place to hold onto, they weren't sure he would've made it."

Libby considered what Ululani was saying.

It seemed that the person with the most need for a change in their perspective was Rob.

"Ululani, I'll see you later," she said as she got to her feet and headed for the door.

"Okay, see you, Libby," the young woman replied as she continued to work on her bed.

She went to the office to look for Rob but he wasn't there. She checked the rest of the inn and he wasn't there either.

"Can I help with anything?" a staff member asked as she entered the kitchen.

"I was looking for Rob."

"Oh he's at home," the woman replied. "He's got a house just up the beach."

"Thanks," Libby said in a rush as she turned and left. She stopped short. "Which direction?"

"North."

She might be overstepping calling on Rob like this, but she needed to tell him what she was thinking.

Christmas was just a few days away and if they wanted to do this properly, they had to do it now.

CHAPTER 17

❄

The walk was longer than she thought, but soon a Tiffany blue colored beach house with white trim came into view.

Libby stood on the sand looking at it.

There was a gate that led in from the beach to a small yard area and she wondered if she should just walk in, or if she should call out to Rob first and let him know she was there.

In the end, the choice wasn't hers to make; he saw her before she had a chance to do anything.

"Libby? What are you doing here?" he asked as he looked at her over the line of fresh laundry. He was shirtless and his hair was pulled back in a low ponytail.

"I came to talk to you."

"Come on in," he said casually as he continued to hang out his laundry.

She let herself in by the gate and came to stand beside him. "Want some help?"

"Sure." He tossed a damp pillowcase at her and smiled. "You can talk while you help me hang these out."

Libby began pinning laundry to the line.

"So I think I've finalized my idea for a different kind of Christmas."

"Oh?" Rob asked as he grabbed a pair of pants from the basket and hung them next to the sheet.

"We need to remember and honor the good. Bad things happen, but good things do too. We need to focus on that. We can each do something that reminds us of the special times we had, at Christmas and otherwise."

Rob stopped what he was doing and turned to look at her. A smile began to spread across his face.

"Kalea used to do this thing … what the Hawaiian people used to do before they celebrated Thanksgiving as we know it, and it happened on the last day of December."

She smiled. "So why don't we do something like that? A day of remembering the best things about our lives. A day to forget all the bad?"

He stared at her, his eyes wandering along her face as if he were looking for something.

"You don't like the idea?" she questioned finally when he remained quiet.

"No," he said calmly. "I do. It's just … it really is the kind of thing Kalea would've loved."

"Rob," Libby said as her hands picked up another pillowcase and held it. "I don't know anything about your wife. I don't know what it must've been like to lose someone you loved that much, but I do know that no one who loved you would ever want you to go through life hurting because of them."

The words stunned even herself as they left her lips. They sunk in as though they were a warning to her too.

She'd been trying to live up to the standards her parents had set instead of making her own. Each year for the holidays she was trying to replicate something that was her mother's and what was expected, instead of doing her own thing.

He laughed softly. "That also sounds like something she'd say."

"Then listen," Libby continued. "Do something that's going to remind you that your wife really loved this time of year. That it meant something to her because of the love she could share and the lives she could touch. You may have lost her physically, but the spirit of what she believed in isn't gone. It's still in you. You kept the inn open in her name. So now run it the way she would want you to. Touch the lives she knew you could."

"What makes you think she believed I could touch lives?" Rob questioned.

"I know that every one of your employees thinks you're amazing. The people you allow to come here, all think highly of you and have good things to say, even if they do think you're a little aloof."

"Aloof? Who said I was aloof?"

"I did," Libby admitted. "I wondered why you were kind of distant. If you were just a big old grump or if there was something more. Then I got to know you and I realized you weren't grumpy. You were just lonely."

"You got that?" he asked as he took a step toward her.

"Yes, I did. The thing is, with loneliness, there's a sure-fire cure."

"What's that?"

"Surround yourself with people and things that make you forget it. That's what I want to do for you and everyone at the inn. I want this Christmas to be a day when we can all forget our troubles and embrace all the good there still is to this life."

He nodded. "Then let's do it. What do you need?"

"First, we need to include all the guests, staff and their families. We can invite them to do the things they love most. Bake their favorite pies or write down their fondest stories or memories to share. Also, why don't we decorate? Not too much, but a festive appearance really does lift the mood and add some cheer. We could ask everyone to pitch in and use *their* favorite decorations. Popcorn garlands, tinsel, lights, whatever reminds them of the best time of their lives even if it isn't necessarily what you might think of as Christmas."

"Libby, I hope they pay you well at your job because you have some pretty good ideas," Rob commented and she blushed.

"Actually, I lost out on a big promotion right before I came here," she admitted.

"You did mention something about that the night we were talking with Nate and Greg."

"Ah, I'm sure I'll get another chance sometime in the future," she replied as she turned from him to hang out the other pillowcase.

It still burned to speak about the disappointment, but she knew that it was something she was going to have to get over.

"Libby?" Rob called as he laid a hand over hers. She stopped what she was doing. "Yes?"

"Don't you think you maybe need to take some of this advice too?" he said in a low voice.

"I know," she admitted hesitantly.

"So why don't we make another deal?" Rob suggested as he removed his hand from hers and she turned to look at him. "I'll let you turn my entire business upside down - do all you've suggested, if you'll throw yourself completely into this plan. I want one hundred percent. Nothing holding you back. No memories of what might have been. If I have to do it then you do too. Agreed?"

She looked at him as a slight embarrassment colored her cheeks. "Agreed."

CHAPTER 18

*R*ob walked her back to the inn afterward. The walk wasn't nearly as long as it was when she'd set out to reach him.

In fact, it seemed to go by far too quickly as they talked.

The first person they met was Naomi. She was walking on the beach collecting shells. It was a past-time she and her husband had enjoyed together.

"Hello, you two? Taking a stroll?" she called out as she spotted them approach.

"Just heading back," Libby said with a smile.

"We were planning something we think you'd enjoy, Naomi," Rob commented. "A day to celebrate."

"Oh?"

"Instead of just Christmas, we want to look at the things that make it really special for each of us and share those things with others," Libby explained. "A day to embrace only the good and forget all the bad."

Naomi looked at her thoughtfully, then a smile began to spread across her face. "I think that's a wonderful idea. In this world we spend far too much time worrying about the negative. My Charlie never did. He always looked at the grass being greener."

"Then you'll participate?" Libby asked enthusiastically. She was eager to see this idea through in reality, and if they could get everyone to jump on board the better it would be.

"I will definitely," Naomi asserted. "I'll see if I can't get some of the others to join us too."

"Do that," Rob answered. "We want staff and guests to come. I plan to make an announcement about it tonight at dinner."

"You should probably get some fliers printed …" Naomi suggested.

"I can do that in my office, but I need someone to design them," Rob said.

"I can design them if you have Adobe or some other software," Libby suggested.

"I'm sure I've got something you can use."

"Then you figure out what to say and I'll work on getting the fliers made." Libby could feel the excitement building. It almost felt like the day of the Hershell presentation, but far less stress and a lot more fun.

"You two sound like a good team," Naomi commented, silencing them both.

"Libby's very talented," Rob said. "She makes things easier."

"Don't mind Rob," Libby said with a chuckle. "He just likes to make his guests feel good about themselves."

"I'd say he's speaking the truth," Naomi agreed.

She could feel her cheeks getting hot. Praise wasn't something Libby was used to, nor something she hardly considered, but the sincerity with which Rob was speaking also made her feel something more.

CHAPTER 19

Christmas Eve came faster than Libby expected and the atmosphere around the inn had completely changed.

Home-made garlands and wreaths hung around the building. The staff were smiling and so were the guests as they helped in the decorating project. Everyone contributed something, whether it was a garland, a food dish or a story.

Every guest also had something to do, and Libby was completely submerged in this lovely new alternative approach to Christmas.

Naomi was spearheading activities in the kitchen, along with the cook. Two other guests were there making some of their family Christmas favorites, while Ululani was making the dough for her mother's cookies.

Her entire family was invited, as well as several other family members of the staff.

"Naomi, everything smells fantastic," Libby commented as she entered the kitchen to see how things were rounding out. The event was starting in an hour.

"Thank you," she said with a smile, "but it isn't all me. The girls have worked so well together."

The cook laughed as did the other women. "We make a good team," the cook replied.

Most of the food was being made by her, but a lot of the dishes were suggested by the guests who knew what they wanted but weren't as skilled at cooking like others.

Everyone was finding their place in this crazy plan and Libby believed it was going to turn out fantastic.

Once she'd checked in with the kitchen and made sure that the music and everything else was ready, she headed to her room to get dressed.

Rob had been a surprise too. He'd really come around to her idea and had ended up being the one leading the decorating.

Now, he was climbing on top of the building with a Santa and Mrs. Claus in shorts and floral print shirts and reindeer with leis around their necks. It looked fun and spectacular all at once.

Libby's dress was bright red and she'd bought a pair of kitten heels for the evening. Her brown hair was swept up in a messy twist and she'd even bothered to do her makeup.

If she was honest, it was the most excited she'd felt about Christmas in years.

SHE MET Rob again on the stairs as she was making her way down to the dining room. She smiled and gave him a small wave as she ascended.

"You look great," he said as he assessed her outfit. He was wearing dark blue jeans and a white ribbed shirt. His hair was down and slicked back.

"So do you," she replied as he held out his arm for her to take it. "Shall we head to the dining room?"

"We shall," Libby answered with a grin, mimicking his formal tone, and the pair began to walk together.

"How are you feeling about this evening?" he asked as they meandered through the lobby. Libby wasn't sure but it almost felt as if Rob was prolonging their arrival.

"Honestly, I'm a bit nervous," she admitted. "I really want this to work and for everyone to have a good time."

"Don't worry. They will," he assured her. "It was a great idea."

"Thanks. I couldn't have done anything in the first place, if you hadn't consented to my hare-brained scheme."

"And I wouldn't be feeling this good if I didn't either."

Libby's face stilled and her heart quickened. "Do you mean that?

He nodded. "I'd forgotten how great this time of year used to be. You reminded me of that. I don't think I can thank you enough."

She blushed. 'Don't mention it. It was my pleasure. And you know, I think I needed this too."

CHAPTER 20

They walked into the dining room to find everyone already gathered together.

Rob left Libby to take his place as MC at the top of the room. He grabbed the microphone already set up with the sound system, and got the festivities started.

"Good evening ladies and gentlemen. Guests, staff and family, I'd like to welcome you to the Kalea Inn's holiday celebration. This evening is a time to remember all the good things we've experienced in our lives, and for one day put aside the unpleasant stuff. I know you must be thinking, 'why?' and the answer is simple really. Why not?"

A soft murmur of laughter rippled across the room.

"Many of us tend to get so caught up in the commercial aspects of Christmas, we overlook the true meaning of the holidays. My late wife used to so love this time of year," he admitted as the room fell silent. "I lost her on Christmas Eve six years ago. I didn't think I'd ever have a happy Christmas again - until now."

Libby stood rapt, listening to Rob pour his heart out. She

marvelled at the way he was able to open up when he'd seemed so closed off when she arrived.

"Then someone reminded me that we need to remember the good. We need to think about the things we tend to forget once we allow the bad stuff to overwhelm us. The bad memories. The misfortunes. The losses. Today, they don't exist. Today we are celebrating only the good."

Libby smiled again as Rob turned to look at her.

"Now I'd like to thank the person who came up with this idea. The person who helped me remember what this time of year truly means. You all know her. She's the one who's been running around making sure you all took part today," he mused. "Libby, thank you - for being you. For being the kind of person who cares about others and who cared enough about all of us here to bring this idea to life. You brought the festive back to this place, and to all of us. Thank you."

Libby's face was red, she knew it. She hadn't expected him to single her out.

Applause filled the room and several encouraging hands touched her shoulder to confirm their agreement with Rob's comments. She didn't know what to say.

Then he passed the mic to the person to his right, and the chorus of thanks and remembrance began.

Everyone sat listening once things got started. People shared their best childhood memories. Some were of Christmas, others of the people they loved.

Naomi shared her most cherished memories with her husband and the funny thing he'd do every Christmas Day. Charlie sounded like an incredible man, and Naomi was smiling with every word she spoke.

That was exactly what Libby wanted. For people to remember only the good.

Greg stood when it was his turn. He looked fondly at his older brother. "The great things I remember most about my life, other than Mom, is my brother, right here," he said as he held out his hand to Nate. "Typically, we honor people when it's too late to tell them how we felt about them. I don't want to do that. I want my brother to know how much he means to me right now, while he's here, and why I'm glad that he's my brother. I couldn't ask for a better sibling. You have always been there to guide me and help me and I'm glad that I can be there for you now. I love you."

Everyone smiled and applauded as the two brothers embraced. Libby dabbed the corner of her eyes as she listened. This was more than she'd expected, but everything she'd hoped for too.

CHAPTER 21

❄

"Finally, the last person to share something this evening. Libby," Rob said, as he handed her the mic.

She was trembling as she took it.

"Thank you," she replied and the mic made a piercing noise. She squinted her eyes as it stung her ears. A moment later the problem was settled. "Thank you," she repeated. "The best times I ever had were with my late parents. They were two of the most loving and committed people I've ever met. They were the glue that held our family together, and I wanted to be just like my mother when I got older. She was the one who made it all work. She was the one who could read us all like a book and solve our problems even before we asked."

"She must've been related to mine," Nate commented and everyone chuckled.

"Maybe," Libby answered. "She seemed to be related to everyone," she mused. "Everyone certainly loved her like she was an aunt or a sister."

Libby was standing in the room, but her mind was somewhere else as she continued.

"Theirs was the love that inspired the kind of love I wanted to have in my life. They set the standard I've aspired to ever since. If it wasn't going to be a love like theirs then I didn't want it. I didn't want to settle for second best or second place. I wanted a love that made you want to be with that person no matter where they went. And while I still might be waiting for that," Libby continued with an ironic chuckle. "I know that it's out there. Real love, the kind that lasts, does exist, and it waits for the right time to make an appearance, but when it does, you'll never forget it."

Applause once again filled the room as she finished her little speech. Her heart was racing in her chest but at least she'd gotten through it. It was amazing. She did presentations for a living but the nervousness never went away, no matter how many times she stood before a crowd to speak.

Once the more personal element was over, it was time for the music and the food. People left their tables and lined up at the buffet to sample the best of Hawaiian cuisine and the mishmash of other favourite personal festive recipes the guests and staff had come up with.

"Libby," Rob called as he pulled her aside. "I just wanted to say thank you again."

"You don't need to," she answered. "You're making too big a deal out of this."

"I don't think so." He gestured around the room. "Look at this. Look at everyone's faces. This is thanks to you. No one else could've done it," he commented.

"She has that effect on people," a familiar voice agreed from behind her. "She always has. Ever since she was a kid."

Libby turned in surprise to find that the words had been spoken by none other than her brother.

CHAPTER 22

❄

*S*he couldn't believe her eyes. There of all people was Andy, backpack slung over his arm and a smile on his face.

"What on earth are you doing here?" she asked in surprise.

"I came to get you," he replied jauntily.

Libby turned to Rob, who was looking from her brother to her and back again.

"It's alright," he murmured, his voice cold once again. "I'll give you two a moment."

"Wait," she called out. "You don't have to go. My brother was just leaving."

She watched as Rob's expression changed. "Your brother?"

"Yes. Andy, this is Rob."

Andy duly took the hand Rob offered in greeting. Libby wasn't happy to see him though.

This was her trip, her escape and he was ruining it by being there. Then, to make matters worse, she saw her sister appear in the doorway. "You brought Eden too?" she asked in disbelief.

"I knew I was going to need reinforcements to get you to come home," he replied. "So brought the best."

"But how did you guys even know where I was?" Libby questioned.

"I think the three of you need to talk. You can use my office," Rob offered, as he pulled the keys from his pocket and handed them to Libby. He stepped closer and whispered in her ear. "Face your problems. Don't run from them."

She looked at him pleadingly, but she knew it was no use. He was right and her siblings had come all this way after all. "Follow me."

Libby led them to Rob's office. She flicked on the light as they entered before she stood in the middle of the room, her arms folded over her chest,

"See that," Eden said as she walked in. "We're in trouble. She's doing the folded arm thing like Mom used to."

"What do you two want?"

"Libs, its Christmas. A time of family and togetherness, like Mom and Dad always wanted," Andy answered.

"It isn't the same without you," Eden added.

"Why? Because there's no one to get the house ready, to cook all the food, clean up after and do your shopping and childminding?" Libby chided. "That's not what Mom and Dad would want, and neither do I."

"We know. We were wrong," Andy said. "We took you for granted and we're sorry for that. It's just ... you always get it done. Everything always comes easier to you and I don't know, I guess we never considered that you'd need help too."

"I worked my butt off on that Hershell project and you took my laptop to New York. I lost my big shot and you acted like it was nothing. A melted candy bar to be replaced. It was my dream and you didn't even care."

"I'm a terrible brother," Andy agreed. "I know that. You disappearing like that really made me realise it."

"Made us all realise it," Eden confirmed. "We understood how much we took you for granted, and how much our lives weren't the same without you being there, and not because you do so much for us, but because you're the sunshine at this time of year, Libby. You're the one who makes it so we don't miss Mom and Dad as much, because we know you've got it all covered by focusing on the good stuff, just the way they'd like."

"But I can't do that anymore," she replied. "I can't do it the way they would want, or what you would want. I need to do it the way I know best and not try to be anyone else. I also need for you guys to play a part. You leave me with everything like I'm a servant, and when you call you just expect me to drop what I'm doing and help you. I know it's my fault for that in a way too. I let you get away with it in the first place, but now I'm not. I've asked for help. I've begged for help. Now, I'm doing what I feel like."

"And you should," Eden said, to Libby's surprise. "You deserve to have the kind of Christmas you want, with the people you want to share it with. I see everything you've done here. When we arrived everyone was talking about this being your idea and they were so excited about it."

"If this is where you'd rather be, then we'll head back home on the first flight tomorrow without you, but if you want to come home, then we've already booked you a flight back. It's all paid for," Andy confirmed.

Libby was about to answer, when something stopped her. What *did* she want? Wasn't it this, what was happening right now - for her family to appreciate her?

She might have helped bring joy to Kalea Inn, but the best

thing for her right now was making things right with her family.

Greg was right. Family needed to show how much they cared for each other now, not later. It was what her parents would have wanted too, and Libby had to admit she missed her siblings. Not speaking to them wasn't natural, especially at this time of year.

She sighed. "Already paid for?"

"Yes," Andy said with a smile as he glanced at Eden."Does that mean you'll come home?"

Libby sighed. "It isn't Christmas without you all either," she admitted. "Despite my desire to escape you guys, being away only made me miss you all the more."

"We missed you too," Eden said as she stepped forward and hugged her tightly.

"I'm sorry little sis," said Andy, joining in. "And I promise we'll make this right. I swear."

CHAPTER 23

"You're all set," the receptionist said cheerily, when Libby checked out out the following morning.

Her flight was leaving in two hours and she, Andy and Eden were headed to the airport.

"Is Rob around?" Libby asked. She hadn't seen him since the night before when she informed him that she would be cutting her trip short in order to go home and spend Christmas with her family.

He'd seemed happy about it, but Libby sensed he was a little disappointed in her too. She'd done so much to help him out and then she was leaving just as things had gotten better.

"He hasn't been in yet today," the young woman replied. "Sorry to hear you're leaving us so soon. Last night was so amazing. Everyone thought so. I wonder if the tradition will continue next Christmas once you're gone?"

"I'm sure it will," Libby asserted. "I'm sure Rob will see to that." She wasn't sure if she meant it, or if she was just trying to convince herself.

She wasn't sure how it happened, but she'd come to really

care about all the people she'd met at Kalea Inn, especially its owner. She'd hate to think that Rob would allow what just happened here; all the beautiful memories and companionship the guests had shared, to fade and for him to fall back into his cloud of melancholy and loneliness.

"Did you want to leave a message for him? I can pass it on when he gets in."

Libby hesitated and then asked for a piece of paper and a pen.

She folded the note and wrote Rob's name on the front.

"Libs, we need to go, the taxi is here," Eden called from the doorway.

"I'm coming," she replied as she walked toward the exit. Then turned back to look at the inn once more.

In a short time, it had made such a big impact on her life. She'd miss it, but maybe sometime in the future she could return?

"Libby," a voice called out then.

"Hey," she smiled broadly, as the older woman walked toward her. Naomi reached up with her frail arms and gave Libby a hug.

"I heard you were leaving," she said. "Take care of yourself OK. Don't forget us."

"I could never forget you," Libby answered as she hugged her again. "I promise, when I get back home I'll give you a call, just to see how you're doing."

Naomi smiled. "I'd like that."

"Libby," her sister called again.

"I have to go," She gave Naomi one final smile. "It was really nice meeting you."

"It was really nice meeting you too. Merry Christmas."

Libby couldn't stop thinking about this trip as the taxi drove them to the airport.

Nothing had turned out the way she thought, but at the same time, it had been infinitely better.

Her only regret was she and Rob not being able to say goodbye. It felt wrong somehow, after everything.

But she thought sadly, there was nothing she could do about that now.

CHAPTER 24

They arrived at the airport on time and Andy took care of checking-in their bags.

"Just a few more minutes and we'll be on our way," Eden mused. "Megan is so happy you decided to come home. She's doing her best to make sure you get a proper Pearson family Christmas when you get there."

Libby's eyes widened. "I hope someone hired a caterer."

"She did actually."

They were still laughing together when a familiar voice called her name.

"Hey," Rob greeted softly, as he got close.

Libby colored, despite herself. "I was hoping I'd get to see you before I left."

Her sister smiled and duly stepped away.

"Well, I wasn't sure if I should say goodbye, but when I got your note I knew I had to." He stepped closer and touched her arm. "I couldn't let you go without saying what's been on my mind …. or in my heart."

Libby looked at him in surprise, and her heart beat louder

in her ears.

"Before you came along, I was sleep-walking through the remainder of my life hoping to never wake up, but you did. You woke me up. You made me feel again. You reminded me of all the good that life still has to offer if we just hold on to it. So that's why I'm here. I'm trying to hold on to some of the good, Libby. You."

Her eyes widened in surprise. "Rob, what are you saying?"

"I'm saying I can't lose this chance. I've been dead inside for so long, and you made me feel alive again. You've made me remember how to feel good about Christmas. I can't let you go back home without letting you know that I care about you. And that I want to see more of you."

"Rob…" She tried to interrupt but he was unburdening his heart and he wouldn't be stopped.

"I know it's crazy. We live so far apart and long distance relationships are tough, but if you're willing to give it a shot, I am too."

An instant smile turned up the corners of Libby's mouth as his words settled in her heart. "Do you mean that?"

"Every word," he answered with a smile of his own. "I know you've decided to go home for Christmas, but if I suggested I maybe come visit you for New Years, would you object?"

She laughed in disbelief. "I wouldn't object," Libby said, still laughing nervously as he stepped closer. "I'd be delighted."

"Do you know you have the best smile….when I see it I can't help but stare at you."

"Is that all?" she asked boldly.

"Actually, it makes me want to kiss you," he continued with a grin. "I just wonder if you'd let me."

"Is that a question?"

"More like a consideration," Rob murmured then softly lowered his lips to hers.

They met somewhere in between. A place between Minnesota and Hawaii, and heaven and earth.

Libby certainly felt as if she were flying as Rob pulled her into his strong arms and held her there.

She was giddy by the time they parted.

An announcement rang over the loudspeaker. Her flight was being called.

"That's me," she chuckled regretfully.

"I'll let you know when I've got all my plans settled," Rob said, as he forced himself to release her.

"If you change your mind, don't tell me OK? It'll be easier that way."

"I'll be there," he said confidently. "You have my word."

She stepped up and kissed him again, a quick one this time as she rushed to meet the others and board the flight.

A FEW MINUTES LATER, Libby was seated and looking out the window of the aircraft as she waited for it to take off.

Christmas had taken on an entirely new meaning for her now. She'd discovered a new way of doing things, and found someone whose heart understood hers.

Better yet, his was leading him to Minnesota for New Years.

The engines hummed to life and she felt excitement build up inside her.

The plane was about to take off, but Libby's heart already had. Her life was changing, she could feel it. And it was all for the better.

All because of her wonderful Christmas escape.

CHRISTMAS BENEATH THE STARS

CHAPTER 1

❄

Hannah Reid loved Christmas.

She loved the cheery feeling in the atmosphere, the twinkling, festive lights and most of all, the sense that at this magical time of the year, anything was possible.

She couldn't add frost or snow to the list though; a born and bred Californian, Hannah wasn't familiar with more traditional wintery Christmas weather.

Yet.

Andy Williams' warm vocals filled the buds in her ears as she reclined in her seat and peered out the window of the aircraft.

Right then, Sacramento lay thousands of miles below in an ocean of darkness and lights. It would be her first holiday season away from home. Her first ever white Christmas.

It was indeed the most wonderful time of the year ...

Hannah hummed the cheery festive tune and glanced down at the cover of the magazine on her lap, a broad smile spreading across her face.

It still felt like a dream.

Discover Wild, one of the biggest wildlife magazines in the country, were sending *her* - Hannah - on assignment.

She ran her hand over the cover shot of a tigress and her cub as they nuzzled together.

It was an amazing photo, one she would have killed to have taken herself.

"Soon," she mused. *Soon it could be my stuff on the cover. All I have to do is get one perfect shot and I'm on my way to a permanent gig with* Discover Wild.

She hugged the magazine to her chest and closed her eyes, relaxing back against the soft leather seat.

IT FELT LIKE JUST A MOMENT, but when Hannah woke it was to the sound of the pilot announcing their descent into Anchorage.

She sat up immediately and looked out the window.

Everything was white!

She'd never seen anything so beautiful. The mountains surrounding the airport were blanketed in thick snow, and a light dusting covered everything else.

She could see the men on the tarmac clearing away the snow, as half a dozen planes in every size - large Boeings to small Cessnas - lay waiting, along with a row of buses to the side.

She wondered which one of those would be taking her to the holiday village she'd chosen as her accommodation while here.

'Nestled deep in the Alaskan wilderness, Christmas World is a true holiday fairytale if ever there was one.

Set amidst lush forest on the South banks of the Yukon River, escape to a magical land where Santa comes to visit every year, and you can find a helpful elf round every corner. Immerse yourself in our idyllic winter paradise and enjoy a Christmas you will never forget ...'

Hannah couldn't wait to experience the true, out and out winter wonderland the online description promised.

Now, the flight was on the ground, but no one was moving. There was a backup of some sort, and passengers were asked to stay on the plane while it was resolved.

Hannah wasn't too bothered; they'd arrived half an hour early in any case, which meant she still had plenty of time before her transfer.

She preoccupied herself on her phone and more online information and picturesque photographs of Christmas World.

The resort homepage featured a group of happy smiling visitors, with various green-and-red clad elves in their midst.

In the background, picture perfect buildings akin to colorful gingerbread houses dusted with snow, framed a traditional town square. It was exactly the kind of Christmas experience Hannah had always dreamed about as a child.

She couldn't *wait* to be there.

CHAPTER 2

Over an hour later, Hannah was still waiting.

In Anchorage International Airport with forty or so other travellers.

Their Christmas World transfer - the so-called 'Magical Christmas Caravan' was late … *very* late.

"You can't be serious," a fellow airline passenger commented nearby. "How much longer are we supposed to wait? Are they going to compensate us for this debacle? It is the resort's transport after all," the disgruntled woman asked.

She was surrounded by three miserable-looking children, while her sullen husband stood in a long line of people trying to find out what was going on.

Hannah had noticed the family on the plane earlier, but now she was getting a better look at them. They were exactly the type of people you'd expect to find on such a jaunt; happy family, blonde-haired and blue-eyed, with their cute-as-a-button kids giddy with excitement about a trip of a lifetime to see Santa.

More decidedly *un*happy faces surrounded the resort's

airport help desk at the moment, but there were plenty of content ones to be found elsewhere too.

A father with his son excitedly perched on top of his shoulders. A serene mother with her sleeping child, and an elderly couple holding hands while they waited for their connection.

It was everything the holidays should be about, Hannah thought; family and loved ones together at the most magical time of the year.

She had been in plenty of airports, but there was something about this one that appealed to her photographer's eye.

The nearby pillars were like pieces of art, almost abstract; though she didn't really know much about art except what she did or didn't like. These were adorned from top to bottom with garlands and white lights. While elsewhere in the terminal, festive wreaths hung on hooks and there were lots and lots of fresh-smelling pine trees.

And of course, then there was the view….

Hannah had taken countless pictures in her life, some to pay the bills and many more for fun. She'd taken portraits, and even the occasional wedding when things were slow between wildlife jobs, but there was something about the outdoors that she loved most of all.

She'd spent her entire life in it after all, had hiked the Quarry trail in Auburn so many times she felt she knew it by heart. Same for the Recreational River, Blue Heron Trail and the Simpson-Reed Trail, and that was just California.

She'd zigzagged her way across America with her collection of trusty Nikon SLR cameras, but she'd never ventured this far north.

The furthest she'd been was Alberta for a wildlife safari

last summer. It was those photos that had opened the door to her current opportunity.

And the reason she was in this snowy picture perfect wonderland right now.

AN HOUR OR SO LATER, and Hannah was peering out the window of Christmas World's transfer coach as Anchorage melted away in a sea of white.

Fresh snow had begun to fall half an hour before, which almost made up for the exorbitant wait.

But at least they were on their way now, and soon Hannah would have a warm lodge, a toasty fire and the most magical Christmas experience awaiting her.

She wondered if there really would be fresh roasted chestnuts available as advertised, and what kind of activities there would be for guests to enjoy when they arrived.

The website listed things like dog-sledding and carolling, plus places to get hot chocolate, Christmas cookies, and a myriad other festive treats.

All of which sounded amazing, especially since she was tired and in sore need of some holiday cheer after such a long travel day.

She imagined the resort town as something like from the movie, *It's A Wonderful Life*, with that close-knit community feel throughout.

Yes, she was here primarily for a career opportunity, but she'd be lying if she said there wasn't the element of living out a fantasy white Christmas too.

Hannah turned back to the window. The snow was falling harder now, and the smile wouldn't leave her face.

She was about to have the best Christmas ever; she could feel it. And she couldn't wait for it to begin.

It's like Christmas morning. The faster you sleep, the faster it arrives.

Isn't that what Mom and Dad always said?

CHAPTER 3

Two hours later, the coach finally arrived at Christmas World to the applause of all the now-deeply disgruntled and exhausted guests.

It was almost four hours past their scheduled arrival time, and darkness had already fallen hours before; just after two in the afternoon when the sun set.

It was now after seven and Hannah was starving.

It took a while to get off the coach. Everyone wanted to get inside the lodge, but were all too tired to make a mad dash for it, which meant they merely shuffled along as they gathered their belongings.

Though once disembarked, the short walk into the lodge heralded even more long lines.

Hannah's group weren't the only new arrivals this evening, it seemed.

"Oh come on," she groaned.

More lines?

She dropped her camera bag on top of her case as she

craned her neck to see as far as the front desk. It was going to be a *long* wait.

"What are they saying up there?" she asked a fellow passenger on the way back from the concierge area.

"They apologized for the delays. Again. It's going to be a couple more hours before our rooms are ready. The hold up with the coaches meant the people checking out were stranded here so things have fallen behind," the older man told her.

"Did they indicate how long of a wait?"

He took a long breath and rolled his eyes. "There's only one person on the desk. By the looks of things, it's going to be a while."

Great.

The man left Hannah to do nothing but wait and take in the madness around her. Everyone looked so exhausted and miserable.

Not exactly a fairytale start.

A porter told everyone to line their bags up along the wall until they were ready to be checked-in.

Hannah left her suitcase, but she wasn't about to leave her camera equipment unattended. She adjusted the strap on her shoulder.

Might be a better idea to just head out and take a look around town instead, maybe take a couple of shots and get a feel for the area?

And perhaps grab a welcome hot chocolate from a cosy cafe…

She gave the long lines one final glance before she stepped out the door and shrugged.

Just because the trip had a poor start didn't mean anything. These things happened in wonderland too.

. . .

Hannah's boot-clad feet made barely a track in the snow-covered street, and she felt a childlike thrill as she heard it crunch beneath her steps.

Her footwear matched the tan-colored fur trimmed parka she wore over her light blue jeans, and she pulled a red knit hat from her pocket and put it on, bunching her dark curly hair above her ears.

It was apparently just a couple of minutes walk to the town square from the hotel.

The lodgings at Christmas World seemed to be made up of five buildings, the main hotel and four oversized log cabins that consisted of multiple rooms, each situated amidst spruces on the way in to the centre of town.

Hannah took a few shots of the area as she walked.

The cabins weren't particularly aesthetic or traditional though, and the only lighting along the way came from inside the illuminated buildings.

A cold wind danced across her face. The air was crisp, almost sweet, and she loved it.

The sky was a deep midnight blue and dots of what looked like a million stars filled it. The clarity was remarkable, like nothing she'd ever seen, and certainly nothing at all like the city sky at home.

Hannah raised her camera lens, and the stars immediately rushed into brilliant focus.

Christmas Beneath the Stars... wait 'til Discover Wild *gets a load of this...*

CHAPTER 4

She snapped several shots of the twinkling night sky before going on her way, anticipating more street lighting to appear as she neared the town, but what she saw was not at all what she'd expected.

Harsh fluorescent floodlights illuminated the area around the square. It almost hurt her eyes it was so bright; and just way too much.

Hannah wandered around the square for a while, peering into window after window, her heart plummeting with each consecutive glance.

This place was *nothing* like she imagined. The town square, though pretty, wasn't in the least bit idyllic or magical.

For one thing, it was practically deserted.

The festive lights, smiling visitors, artisan shops and cheerful elves promised in the promo material were all absent.

There was a shabbily dressed (and grumpy-looking) Santa sitting by a cabin and gaudy Christmas tree nearby, taking pictures with unhappy children who weren't at all fooled or indeed impressed by his dingy, fake beard and oversized Santa suit.

Hannah kept walking. Surely there had to be more to Christmas World than *this*?

Eventually, she spied a simple wooden cabin with a red and white sign marked 'Santa's Post Office', which looked interesting.

A bored-looking elf sat just inside it, his head resting on his hand. "Merry Christmas. Leave a letter for Santa. Get one back on Christmas," he recited jadedly.

Her spirits plummeting, Hannah quickly moved on and headed to a nearby 'craft gift' store.

But once again she was disappointed. There were no hand-painted artisan reindeer, woodcraft or any locally-made creations at all.

Instead, she found plastic Santas and inflatable Rudolph toys; the same that could be found at any gift shop in America over the holiday season.

There was *nothing* special about what was on offer there, no souvenirs at all of Christmas World for visitors to take home and treasure.

She frowned. Maybe she was in the wrong area and there was somewhere else - somewhere better?

"Excuse me?" she asked the youthful-looking shopkeeper scrolling through his phone. The kid didn't even look up from the device. "Where are the craft shops? This can't be the only one. Right?"

The kid remained expressionless as he answered. "No."

"No?" she questioned incredulously.

"No." He looked at her as if she belonged in Special Ed class.

She grimaced at a plastic reindeer. "Thanks for nothing," she muttered as she walked away.

She'd had enough for today.

Hopefully her room was ready by now.

CHAPTER 5

Hannah returned to the main lodge to find the reception area now emptying out.

Most of the other guests had been shown to their rooms, and only her belongings remained lined up against the wall.

Thank goodness for that at least. She collected her stuff and headed to check-in.

She'd been assigned an upstairs room, and it was... small.

Hannah expected it to be cosy but not stifling. It reminded her more of a cruise ship cabin than a hotel room.

There was a single bed, a rug and a wooden chair in one corner of the room alongside a standing lamp.

A bedside table was positioned on the right of the bed with a smaller lamp, alarm clock, and telephone.

There was no TV but she expected that. This kind of destination was all about outdoor activities and fun, not lounging around your room watching cable.

What Hannah didn't expect though was a *picture* of a blazing fire, instead of a fire itself.

But perhaps that was understandable too, what with safety code …?

Still, it was disappointing.

She set her bag on the bed and her stomach growled.

She was still hungry and hadn't actually thought to get anything while she was out.

Nor seen anywhere to tempt her either.

She left her equipment on the bed, grabbed her purse and hurried from the room before it got too late.

Downstairs, she picked up a cold tuna sandwich and a Coke; the best the in-house restaurant could do. Apparently the kitchen closed at eight, and there would be no hot meals until morning.

Hannah couldn't believe it. Still, her rumbling stomach was thankful of *something* at least.

Even so, she decided to head back into town and find a place there. She'd be hungry again in half an hour if she didn't get something else to top-up the sandwich.

She hadn't been away long; half an hour to an hour, maybe a little more, but when she returned to the town square there was … nothing.

The area was now shuttered and in darkness; those awful lights the only thing that remained.

Santa was gone. The post office and souvenir store were closed, along with every other retail unit in the area.

The café? In complete darkness. Even the lights on the Christmas tree at the head of the square were turned off.

So much for winter wonderland. What is this miserable place?

If this was what *real* Christmas was like, Hannah was beginning to suspect she hadn't been missing much.

CHAPTER 6

Her neck and back were aching when she woke the next morning.

Despite an exhausting day's travel, she'd spent most of the night before tossing and turning on the lumpy mattress.

She was also *freezing*.

The radiator in her room was obviously broken, so Hannah spent the night wrapped in a cocoon made out of her bedsheets.

She shuffled to the window. It was still dark out.

"When does the sun come up in this place?" she wondered aloud.

She moved then to the ensuite bathroom, and a few minutes later an ear-piercing scream leaped from her lips as freezing water connected with her skin.

Seemed the water heater wasn't working either!

Hannah checked her camera equipment before she went downstairs for breakfast, lining up all her lenses and hardware and checking everything before she went out.

Once she was dressed, and the camera stuff repacked, she headed to the restaurant for breakfast.

Scrambled eggs, bacon and toast with tea and juice was welcome, but bland and needed a lot of salt and black pepper to make it edible.

She tried to not harp on the growing number of disappointments she was finding at Christmas World, but it was difficult.

There were just so many!

However, she had to remind herself that this trip wasn't just about enjoying the holiday village, ultimately it was about work, and she was determined to get the job done regardless of her dissatisfaction.

Once she got out into the wild, things would surely improve.

SHE WALKED BACK in to town to find someone who could shed some light on the best vantage points nearby to spot and photograph the Northern Lights.

It was pretty apparent last night that the artificial street lighting here gave off way too much light pollution for anyone to spot the phenomenon from the town.

Hannah zipped up her jacket and headed back out with two bags of equipment; her usual camera bag and another containing additional lenses.

She saw a line of people forming just up ahead as she passed a sign that read SLED & SLEIGH RIDES.

Hmm... The idea of an actual sleigh ride through the snow, pulled by genuine reindeer was so tempting. She'd always wanted to experience that.

"Wanna take a ride?" a nearby attendant asked her. She

was pleasant, but Hannah got the feeling that the woman wasn't very enthusiastic about being there.

She was dressed as an elf but she had to be at least sixty years old. She actually reminded Hannah of her grandmother.

"Are those ... real reindeer?" she asked in an almost child-like tone, her anticipation building.

The woman chuckled. "Yes, they are. Would you like to take a ride? It's only fifty dollars. It takes you into the forest around town and a little further north too."

"North?" Hannah questioned. "Could you see the aurora borealis from up there?"

"Maybe," the woman shrugged. "The lights can be a bit unpredictable. They happen when they want to. So what about that ride?"

Hannah contemplated the prospect for a moment. "Sure. I'll take it. I just need to check something first," she added.

There was an information desk close by too.

If anyone would know where best to find the Northern Lights someone there surely would. That way, if the sleigh ride took her close enough, she could get her shots and enjoy some fun at the same time.

She approached the kiosk.

"Hi there," Hannah greeted with a smile as she walked up to the tourist information window.

"Hi. You, uh ...want to write a letter to Santa?" a young man questioned with a raised brow. It was the same bored kid Hannah had seen the evening before. He caught himself a second after saying it. "Sorry. I mean, Christmas World Information - how can I help?"

She chuckled lightly. The man in red she saw the night before was no Santa, and even if he was, she wouldn't write to him. "I need a local guide. I want to go see the aurora borealis." She smiled.

The elf looked at her, confused. "Aurora borealis?"

"Yes," Hannah replied. "You know…the Northern Lights?"

"I know what you mean," he replied. "I just don't know anyone who can help you. The lights happen when they want to. No one can be sure when. You might see them a bit further north maybe, but where exactly, I dunno. I've never actually seen them myself."

She blinked in surprise. "But you live around here, don't you? How can you not know where to find them?"

He shrugged. "I don't really have any reason to leave town. Everything is here."

Hannah sighed. This truly was just getting better and better …

CHAPTER 7

"OK thanks anyway," she muttered. "Have a nice day."

She wandered back to the sleigh ride area only to be met by a very long line of waiting people.

Nearby, a group of husky dogs skidded away, with a group sitting happily in the sled behind them.

But there were so many people ahead of her for the reindeer ride, and with the length of time it took for one group to go around and come back, Hannah figured it could well be *hours* before she got her turn.

She stood in the line for a few more minutes before she got tired of it.

"This is ridiculous," she muttered. The man in front of her turned back in jaded agreement.

There was no point in just standing around for ages, wasting her day. There *had* to be a better way to get out into the forest to find the phenomenon, and if it meant finding it on her own, then so be it.

Hannah marched back to the information desk. "Where can I rent a snowmobile?" she demanded.

The attendant looked at her as if she were annoying him and Hannah resisted the urge to give him some Californian sass.

She didn't know why she was surprised though. What was poor customer service when it came to this place? Everything about it was lacklustre and disappointing.

"There's a place over on the other side of town," he droned.

"How much?"

"Twenty bucks an hour, I think."

"Thank you" Hannah replied imperiously, before hurrying away in the direction he pointed.

She had a snowmobile to catch.

Fifteen minutes later, she was packing her equipment onto the back of a fluorescent green Polaris.

The attendant gave her a matching helmet for safety.

"Are you sure you can handle that thing?" the young guy asked.

"Yeah, I'm sure," she scoffed, as she put the helmet on and started it up.

She turned the heavy machine around and headed north, thankful to be leaving the dreary town and letting those garish spotlights fade into the background.

They spoiled everything. The few shots she'd taken the night before were horrible. Overexposed and distorted.

The engine revved in Hannah's ears as she raced across the sea of white. There were several trees on the path but they were so well-dispersed it made navigation easy.

The light was beginning to come up and she was sure that if she traveled far enough she'd find the lights on her own once darkness hit again later. She just wasn't sure how far, but knew to keep careful track of where she was going just in case.

She'd hiked enough and lost her way enough back home to know what to do.

Though Alaska was different. It was dark twenty hours of the day, and of course mostly white on the ground, which meant keeping track was a little more difficult, but not impossible.

Thanks to the stars.

Her late father had taught Hannah from an early age how to find her way by the stars.

All she had to do was find the North Star. It was at the tip of the Little Dipper's handle, the first constellation her dad had ever shown her.

She felt a pang, missing him afresh.

He would love it here out in the forest. This is just his kind of thing.

She smiled to herself. Her father had been an adventurer. He'd sparked it inside of her and it was a flame that had never been extinguished.

She'd taken him on many of her wildlife shoots in return. It was only later in life that he'd stopped going. When rheumatoid arthritis started it was difficult for him to accept that he could no longer do the things he used to.

And while he was now longer around to do the things they loved, Hannah still could, and she would.

It was her dream for so long. She wasn't going to let anyone or anything stop her.

She was going to find one of the world's most amazing natural phenomena.

Hanah would stay out here in the snow, beneath the sky for as long as needed, until she could capture the aurora borealis in a way that would immortalize it forever.

No matter what.

CHAPTER 8

Alaska cold was like none other Hannah had ever experienced, however.

Her breath didn't come out as mist, but as an actual cloud before her eyes.

Thankfully she had goggles to protect them from the blinding glare of the sun bouncing off the blanket of white.

The tundra was spectacular though; the snow drifts all-encompassing. There didn't seem to be a single spot uncovered out there.

The shifting winds drew patterns in the snow like a finger. It all looked like a patchwork quilt from the distance, and Hannah kept stopping the snowmobile to photograph the almost surreal landscape.

The sun appeared just after eleven am, but by three-thirty it was setting again.

Hannah took as many photos as she could during daylight hours, but of course it was in darkness that she'd have the best hope of tracking down the auroras.

Now the sky was truly dazzling, studded with stars that looked like diamonds overhead.

She got off the snowmobile and set her goggles and helmet aside to just look up and stare at it.

She wandered slightly, allowing her feet to carry her as her eyes remained focused above her.

Just incredible ...

She stayed there immobile, completely oblivious to what may lurk in the trees or in which direction she was walking. She just kept following the patterns in the stars, letting them be her guide.

I should have come here long ago. It's like an untouched land ... as if nothing has changed here since the world began.

Eventually Hannah returned to the snowmobile and placed her goggles and helmet back on before heading north.

The attendant said that was the way to go, so that was where she was going.

An hour later she was further north, but still no closer to spying the aurora borealis.

She'd searched in every direction she could think of and still there was nothing.

Could a phenomenon hide? Wasn't it supposed to be right there, for all to see?

Hannah flipped her goggles up over her helmet and looked around her. Where else could she look?

This was her future, the biggest opportunity of her professional life; she needed to find the Northern Lights soon.

She *had* to.

She took a few more shots of the twinkling night sky, but

another hour or so later there was still no sign of what she'd come to see.

She sighed and leaned on the handles of the snowmobile. What was she going to do? Clearly she was in the wrong place, or the conditions weren't right, or *something*.

The problem was she needed to figure this out. She wasn't going to get another opportunity like this. It could make or break her career.

She decided to give herself one more hour before giving up.

But still, there was still nothing.

Hannah set her helmet on the handle of the snowmobile and took a long, deep breath.

She felt tears of frustration sting her eyes, but quickly pushed them back.

"You are not gonna panic," she told herself. "There's always tomorrow. You'll be able to find *someone* in town who knows about the auroras, and they can point you in the right direction. You are not a quitter. You never have been. Just get back to town and start afresh tomorrow."

She gave the sky one last glance before she put the helmet back on and restarted the snowmobile.

The engine had just stirred to life when tiny flecks of snow began to fall, immediately lightening Hannah's mood.

I really could just stay in this picture postcard forever...

She took a few artistic shots of snowflakes against the sky with the moon and stars in the background, before she reluctantly put the camera away, and manoeuvred the snowmobile round to head back.

The weather began to come down even harder and a few minutes later, her vision was almost completely obscured.

In the blizzard, Hannah truly couldn't tell where she was going and had nothing to guide her.

Snow clouds hid her trusty stars, and every tree she passed seemed just like the other.

She stopped the vehicle to help gather her bearings, trying not to panic. The snow was coming down way too hard. It was a risk to keep going so better to just wait a little until it eased off.

Hannah sat impatiently on her snowmobile for a half hour or so until the heavier snowfall eventually lightened.

When all was clearer she once again tried to find her way back to the resort village.

But her earlier tracks were completely gone by now, the fresh snowfall obscuring her only means of finding her way back.

Things truly were just going from bad to worse ...

CHAPTER 9

Hannah's gaze searched frantically around. Which way?

She bit the inside of her cheek as she contemplated one direction over another.

She drove slowly and with trepidation, hoping for some confirmation that she was going the right way, until finally passing a clump of trees that looked familiar.

Relieved she was on the right track, she turned up the throttle, eager to get back now.

She was getting hungry, not to mentioned wet, tired and *cold*.

In her haste, she steered the vehicle round a cluster of trees, going far too fast.

Hannah felt the big machine begin to slide, right in the direction of a large snow-covered mound of ... something.

Her eyes grew large as she realized she was going to hit it. Swerving in panic, she felt the snowmobile begin to give way and topple over, and like a mother protecting her children, she reached for her camera bag to save it.

She squeezed her eyes shut as she tumbled free of the snowmobile and landed awkwardly in the snow.

Feeling a sharp pain in her wrist, Hanna cried out, her hand clasped around it. She hissed, the pain of it throbbing through her as she rocked back-and-forth.

It took several minutes before the pain eased enough for her to release her hold.

With the other hand, Hannah unbuckled her helmet and removed it so to assess the damage to herself, the snowmobile, but most importantly, her camera equipment.

She felt no pain anywhere else except for her wrist, and for that much she was thankful.

Her cameras seemed to be all in good order too; however, the snowmobile on its side half-buried beneath a snow mound was not so lucky.

The problem was, with her injured wrist, there was no way she was going to be able to dig it out on her own to get back.

Which meant she was stranded. Deep in the forest in the darkness amid falling snow - all on her own.

Hannah looked around again as panic began to creep into her heart. She grabbed her phone from her bag and began to dial the number for the Christmas World lodge.

No service.

She tried again, but the call still refused to go through. Her fears began to grow the longer the line refused to connect.

She was stranded in the dark, in the middle of nowhere without a single way of communicating her situation to anyone.

What was she going to do? She had enough snacks and water to last a couple of hours at least, and her clothes were thick enough to keep her warm enough for a while ... but she had nowhere to shelter if the snow started falling again, nor knew anywhere nearby to take refuge.

Hannah got to her feet, her hand cradling her aching wrist. She turned around, searching for some kind of magic answer to her problem, but there was nothing.

No sign of anything. No smoke rising into the air, no sound except a light wind in the trees.

CHAPTER 10

❋

"Hello?" she called out impulsively. "Anyone there?"
Silence.

Her heart began to stampede.

Be calm, Hannah. Be calm.

She wandered clear of the tree line.

Maybe if she got into a clearing she might be able to see better? Perhaps there was something on the way that she'd missed…

Her feet sunk into the snow up as far as her calves. She shivered, more out of fear now than cold.

Then she thought she heard something in the distance. Something faint, and her hearted quickened even more.

"Hello!" she called out again, this time much louder. "Anyone?"

Her eyes searched the tundra for some sign of which direction the noise was coming from.

Then she heard it again, a little louder this time. Then again, and this time she could make out what it was.

Dogs barking.

Her heart began to fill with hope. If there were dogs out here, then there must be somewhere close by for her to find safety.

Hannah cupped her good hand against her mouth and yelled as loudly as she could. "Hello!"

She spotted it then, a sled led by six husky dogs and a single driver.

She moved towards it, waving her good hand frantically as she continued to call out.

It took a minute before she was noticed, but mercifully the sled eventually started in her direction.

Her heart almost leaped out of her chest with relief.

She was safe.

Hannah walked toward the stranger, who would surely help get her back to civilization.

"Hey there, can you help me? I had an accident," she said, approaching the stranger, just before another thought stuck her.

Please, please don't be a serial killer...

CHAPTER 11

Hannah's heart was still beating hard in her chest, as the sled driver approached.

She dismissed the fear as she glanced at the adorable huskies leading it. There were six altogether, and she stepped closer as the dogs came to a stop.

Her eyes drifted from the animals to their master. A guy was standing on the back of the sled, an earflap hat on his head and large goggles covering his eyes.

Breath billowed from his lips as he looked at her. Then he stepped off the sled and raised the goggles from his face.

Hannah's heart fluttered.

This guy was made to be photographed. The camera would devour him (along with likely every woman who got an opportunity).

His face was tanned with an angular jaw, full lips, light green eyes, and she could see golden-blonde hair peeking out from beneath his hat.

He was tall too, at least a foot taller than she was, and dressed in a dark parka and thick ski pants.

If she had to guess, he wasn't from around these parts, not with that tanned complexion, but he'd definitely dressed for the weather.

"What happened here?" he asked as he approached. He removed his gloves and stuffed them into his pocket. "Anyone else out here with you?"

His question did cause Hannah a little apprehension. Was she alone?

Stop ... overactive imagination.

"No, it's just me. I was trying to get back to town and I took a turn too quickly and my snowmobile turned over in a snowbank," she explained. "It's back there in the trees."

"It happens. I'm Bruno. Bruno Locke," he introduced himself.

"Hannah Reid," she replied. Forgetting herself, she instinctively flexed her wrist to take his hand, but the moment she did, a shot of pain ran up her arm.

She grabbed at her wrist again to soothe it.

Please, don't be broken. Don't be broken.

"You OK?" Bruno questioned.

She grimaced. "I hurt my arm when I fell off the snowmobile. It's nothing."

He stepped closer and took her hand. She could see the slight shadow of a mustache over his lip and she averted her eyes, and instead tried to focus on what he was doing with her arm.

He moved her wrist around, first to the left and then the right, and finally up and down. She hissed her displeasure as fresh pain coursed through her.

He cocked an eyebrow. "Sounds like more than 'nothing' to me," he commented, then glanced at the snowmobile, emblazoned with the Christmas World logo. "You staying at the resort?"

Hannah nodded.

"It's late. Better get you back soon." He released her hand and started walking to where she'd fallen. "What were you doing all the way out so far this late?"

Hannah grimaced. "I was actually trying to see the aurora borealis, but I couldn't find it."

His brow wrinkled slightly. "The auroras? You won't see anything out this way. Didn't anyone tell you?"

"No," she said through gritted teeth. "I tried to find someone to show me but the people in that ... town didn't seem to have a clue. They told me to head further north, so here I am."

"Folks who live up here with the auroras don't find them as impressive as those who come from far away." Bruno looked her over. "And by the looks of you, I'd say you come from very far away."

"California," she informed him. "I'm out here on a work assignment."

He walked ahead of her, his long strides allowed him to move a lot faster than Hannah. He looked over his shoulder. "What do you do?"

"Photographer," she replied.

He reached the snowmobile and Hannah occupied herself with collecting her scattered belongings, while he worked on getting her transportation free.

She stood watching as he began to dig the snowmobile out. It didn't take him long with two perfectly working hands, though it did take a little more effort to get it upright again.

"Do you need help?"

"I think my hands are better than yours at this point," he

replied. "I just need to get a little leverage."

Bruno lowered himself and used his body weight to push the snowmobile over. It took him a couple of tries, but eventually he got it done.

"Thanks." Hannah stepped closer and inspected the snowmobile with him. It seemed OK on the surface, the body undamaged at least.

Bruno got into the seat and tried to start it.

The engine made a strange sound but didn't turn over. He tried again. Same thing.

"Sounds like your engine's flooded," he commented. "There's no way you're getting back to town on this thing."

"So what do I do? I can't just stay out here…"

He smiled, a wide grin that displayed perfectly even, polished white teeth, and dimples to boot.

"Well, you definitely need to get someone to look at that wrist soon. I can give you a ride back." Bruno got off the snowmobile, took the keys out of the ignition and handed them to her. "You staying at one of the lodges?"

"Yes, the main lodge at Christmas World. The most *un*-Christmassy place you can possibly imagine," she muttered, rolling her eyes. "Honestly, it's more like somewhere you want to *avoid* if you want to retain your Christmas spirit. But unfortunately, I'm stuck there until I get this job done."

Bruno nodded silently. "Most un-Christmassy place huh?"

"Yes. You've heard of Christmas World I take it?"

"Yeah, I've heard of it. It was quite a place years ago but now it's something else."

"Ha! *That's* an understatement," Hannah scoffed as she did her best to get her haversack and camera bag over her shoulder. "I came here expecting this amazing once in a lifetime festive experience," she admitted. "I thought it was going to be the Christmas I never had. And I was right - but in *all* the *wrong* ways."

Her heart sank as the words left her lips. She didn't truly admit to herself how disappointed she was by Christmas World until she'd uttered the words out loud.

She looked at her feet as they sank into the snow. "I thought I was going to have my first perfect white Christmas, while also getting to experience one of the world's most amazing natural phenomena. Instead, I was met with the polar opposite. Plus I can't seem to even find the Northern Lights."

"Let me," Bruno offered. He slid both bags from her shoulders and started walking toward the sled. "I'm so sorry you were disappointed."

She shrugged. "It doesn't matter I guess. I'll make the most of it. If I get the shots I came for, then it'll be worth it."

"What if you don't? That wrist doesn't look so good."

"Then I'm looking forward to the *worst* Christmas imaginable, cooped up in Scroogeville while I wait for this to heal." She waved her injured hand slightly. "This is nothing. Just a little bump. I'm sure it'll be fine in a day or two." She looked back at the snowmobile. "Though I can't just leave that there, can I? The rental place is gonna want it back."

"I've saved the location on GPS. They'll be able to send someone to retrieve it. Now, take a seat," Bruno declared. He'd cleared a place in front of him on the sled for her to sit.

Hannah patted the dogs and they licked her hand. Two of them were black and white, another two were copper-red and white and the last two were paler versions of the ones before. They were all so adorable with their pale eyes. One had heterochromia: one eye pale blue and the other ochre.

"These guys are so sweet," she stated as she knelt beside

the dogs and gave them an additional pat on the head each. They jumped up playfully. "I always wanted dogs like these," she added.

"I always wanted them too," Bruno agreed. He smiled. "That's why I got them."

Hannah got up and walked to the sled, lowering herself onto it.

"Pull the blanket over your legs. It'll get pretty cold being closer to the snow."

She did as Bruno suggested. "What're their names?"

"The three on the left are Bonbon, Snicker and Tootsie. The other three are Caramel, Chocolate and Vanilla," he told her, as he gave the command and the dogs started off running.

Hannah chuckled. "You have a sweet tooth?"

"Just a little. How could you tell?"

She took the liberty of peeking over her shoulder at him. The goggles were back in place but it did nothing to detract from the fact that he was a seriously good-looking guy. She wondered how he'd ended up all the way out there in the wild.

"Let's get you home."

"Whoopee," Hannah said lackluster. "Christmas World here we come."

She wrapped her arms around her knees deep in thought, as the tundra began to fly by.

She had no idea how she was going to explain the accident to the attendants at the rental place, or the additional eighty bucks she owed them for staying out far longer than she'd promised.

No Northern Lights. No pictures. Busted snowmobile. Busted wrist.

Could this trip truly get any worse?

CHAPTER 12

❄

The town was unsurprisingly, once again in darkness when they approached.

A deep sigh left Hannah's lips at the sight of it. Didn't anyone ever tell whoever ran Christmas World that activities and lights - *especially* during the holidays - might be good for business?

What was it with these people?

"See what I mean?" she commented to Bruno archly. "This is supposed to be a magical, festive destination, yet the place is in complete darkness before anyone even has a chance to get out and enjoy it. It's just so ... *depressing*! Especially when it's dark up here so many hours already, and when you look out your window there's only more darkness. To say nothing of those tacky fluorescents in the square..."

Bruno murmured agreement as he steered the dog sled up to a darkened building.

"Wait here," he instructed. "I'll go get a doctor."

Hannah looked at him surprised. "Where will we find a doctor now? Everywhere's closed."

He removed his hat and goggles, and she realized that she was right about his model good looks. His tousled golden-blonde hair fell just above his ears. He looked like a Norse god.

She swallowed hard.

"I know a guy, Dr. Morgan who lives out this way. I'll go get him and bring him back." He switched on a lamp strapped to the back of the sled. "So you won't be alone in the dark," he added as he flashed a smile. "And the dogs will be here to keep you safe. You don't have to worry though, we don't really have any crime up here. Everyone knows everyone else so it doesn't leave much room for mischief."

With that, he strode off into the darkness and Hannah remained with the dogs.

The pups began playing the moment they were left on their own. They tumbled over each other and wrestled like children. She smiled. So far, they (and Bruno) were the best thing about this place.

She got to her feet with some pain and effort; her wrist was throbbing terribly as she moved, and she aggravated it even more when she tried to get up from her low seating.

Hannah held it to her chest as she looked again around the deserted town. Why did they even *bother* to promote this place as a vacation destination?

Like Jurassic Park at Christmas, she grumbled. Minus the dinos.

Nearby the reindeer were milling around in their pen. The wind was blowing gently through the trees and the smell of spruce filled the air.

Though if they *did* do something with the place it could be amazing....

Hannah turned back to focus her attention on the dogs.

They were a friendly little bunch and didn't seem alarmed or wary of her at all, not even with Bruno gone. They seemed to like her as much as she liked them.

Minutes more passed and soon their owner was returning, with another man beside him. "Doc, this is Hannah, the guest I told you about."

The hefty man smiled at her. "The little snow-racer," he mused. He stepped toward her and looked at how she was cradling her arm. "Let's get you inside so I can get a better look at what we're dealing with."

CHAPTER 13

In truth, Hannah was a bit shocked by what she found inside the town Medical Centre.

Christmas World in general might have been a dud, but their healthcare facilities were obviously top notch.

Unfortunately for Hannah, that didn't necessarily mean anything good for her.

"It's a sprain, and a bad one. Grade Two. This means that some of the palmar ligaments have partially been torn," Dr. Morgan explained. "You're going to have some loss of function, and you're going to need to have your hand immobilized in a splint for at least a week." He went over to a supplies cabinet and began to unpack items from it. "I'll give you some stretching exercises to help regain your mobility."

Hannah's heart fell through the floor. "Doctor … are you telling me I won't be able to use my hand at all?"

This couldn't be happening. If she couldn't use her shooting arm then there was no way she was going to complete her photography assignment.

"Isn't there any way to speed up this process? I mean, a

painkiller or something? I really need to use my arm. It's work."

"I'm sorry. There's truly no way to rush these things. It takes as long as it takes."

Hannah was silent as Dr. Morgan wrapped her arm.

None of it seemed real. She couldn't locate the auroras, she had a sprained wrist, and was marooned in the worst 'holiday destination' imaginable.

This has to be some kind of joke. Or definitely a bad dream.

When the doctor was finished, she returned to the reception area where Bruno was still waiting.

"So what's the verdict?"

"A bad sprain," Dr. Morgan answered.

"At least it's not broken."

"No, just injured enough to ruin everything I came here for," Hannah grumbled. "I better get back to the lodge and get a message to the magazine, let them know what happened and that I can't complete the assignment."

She strode toward the door, determined to walk off her disappointment and frustration.

Though Bruno stepped in front of her, and touched her arm gently.

"Hannah, I don't think you should go back to the lodge yet," he stated. "The magazine can wait until tomorrow when you've had time to process what's happened. You're upset right now; not the best state of mind to figure out what you need to."

"I'll be fine," she protested.

"Look, I know a place. Let me take you for some hot chocolate to cheer you up? You've had a lousy day."

"Bruno…"

"I won't take no for an answer," he insisted.

He flashed a grin in her direction, and Hannah knew it would be rude to refuse, especially when he'd been so kind already.

Not to mention she couldn't resist a smile like that even if she tried.

CHAPTER 14

❄

Bruno led her outside, and back to the sled. He drove it a little way across the town square to one of the few places with lights on; a tiny café with no more than six tables inside.

It had large picture windows lined halfway with a short white curtain. Ornate electric starlights hung at the top, casting pretty light patterns on the walls.

They left the dogs outside, and upon entering, Hannah was surprised to find that a proper working fireplace was providing most of the heat. Two large, plush chairs sat on a cosy rug by the hearth.

A woman stepped out from behind a counter the moment they entered. She had pepper and salt hair that hung in a thick braid over her shoulder. Her skin was olive, and there was such youthful vigor in her movements that it made Hannah smile.

"Hey, Bruno. I haven't seen you here in a while. How's your dad?" she asked, as he attempted to help Hannah out of her coat. "What happened here?" she added, indicating her sling.

"Thanks Gretta. Dad's good. I know it's late, but my friend here needs some of your famous hot chocolate." He flashed that grin again, one that would melt any woman's heart.

"Famous, huh?" she replied, an amused twinkle in her eye. "You can take that table over by the window." She looked at Hannah. "You hungry sweetheart?"

"Starved."

"Then I'll bring you guys a menu too. Get yourselves comfortable; I'll be right back."

They sat at the table and Hannah stared down at her wrist. She was so disappointed, but for Bruno's sake tried to distract herself. "She seems lovely."

"Yep. Gretta owns this place and she is. Her family has been in this area for two hundred years. They were some of the original tribes in the area before it became settled."

"That's amazing."

"The cafe is here since before I was born," he continued. "The family have been taking care of the people round here ever since, and the café was just Gretta's addition to that legacy. Plus, she makes the best food between here and Anchorage." Then his expression fell. "Hannah, I'm afraid I owe you an apology."

She frowned. "What? You don't need to apologize for anything. None of this is your fault."

"Actually it is," he replied.

She stared at him, confused. "What are you talking about?"

"There's something I should tell you. When you asked if I'd heard of Christmas World, and I said I did. Well … it's a little bit more than that. I own it."

Her eyes widened, stunned. "You … own it?"

"Pretty much. I'm the CEO. I took over running the company last year when I came back from the military. My father was sick and he passed on the management to a third party while I was away, but when he got worse I took early leave to come home."

Her jaw dropped as she listened. Then she snapped it closed and played off the action with a lick of her lips.

"I...I don't know what to say. I'm kind of embarrassed obviously. I would never have said what I did if I..."

"Knew?" Bruno finished. He smiled. "It's alright. You were just being honest. Besides, I needed to hear it. I can't pretend this place is anything like it used to be."

Hannah leaned closer. "What happened? Forgive me for being nosy, but this isn't at all what I imagined and definitely isn't what's advertised. I don't want to believe you'd trick people into coming here, so something must have happened to turn the place into...well into this."

"Here you go," Gretta interrupted politely. She set two large mugs in front of them, filled with rich chocolate, whipped cream and marshmallows on top. It smelled divine.

"Thanks, Gretta. This looks great," Bruno smiled. "It's always great here," he said to Hannah.

"I wish there were more people who thought so," the woman replied glumly. "Things have been so slow this year."

"I know."

Hannah could see the disappointment in Bruno's expression.

"Things will probably pick up closer to Christmas though," Gretta assured him quickly. "Every town has its ups and downs. We've made it through worse and we will make it through this one." She patted his shoulder comfortingly. "I'll let you both decide on what you want to eat."

Gretta left them and Bruno turned back to Hannah.

"See, it isn't just you who thinks this place isn't what it used to be. Everyone does. The company my dad had taking care of things made some big mistakes. Letting staff go to reduce costs, closing early to reduce expenses, and raising prices on retail space to increase profit. What it did was force all of the artisans out, left local people without work, and turned Christmas World into … a crackerjack house." He sipped his chocolate and set it aside. "They thought that 'recreating daylight' with those floodlights you hate was more cost-effective than the lighting system already in place."

"They sure got that wrong."

"Yes, they did. So I do feel personally responsible for the awful time you're having here. And the guys who rented the snowmobile really should've given you a map too, but they sent you off unprepared. You came here for a dream Christmas but got a nightmare instead."

Hannah's gaze fell to the table. She felt so bad for him and doubly terrible for complaining so vociferously earlier. He'd already done so much to help her today, and he didn't even know her

"Truly it's not your fault." She placed her good hand on his to get his attention. "Maybe my expectations were just too high. Yes, things might have gotten off to a bad start around here. But I have a feeling they'll get better."

He met her gaze then and something … Hannah couldn't be sure what, passed between them.

She felt her cheeks grow warm, worried that she'd overstepped, then pulled her hand away and picked up her oversized mug with her good arm.

She raised a toast. "Here's to starting over."

Bruno smiled and raised his in return.

CHAPTER 15

*H*annah regarded Bruno over the brim of her oversized cup, still feeling like such a heel for what she'd said, and the obvious discomfort it had brought him.

"Hey," she said softly then. "I know you said I don't have to, but I really do want to apologise too. I'm very sorry for what I said about this place. I had no right to go off on you like that before. I should've just kept my big mouth shut. I feel like I insulted you and your family business and that was not my intent. It really wasn't."

He smiled at her. "You told the truth. As I said, I appreciate honesty and I share your views. This isn't the type of place people would want to come back to, which is probably why they haven't."

"I heard what Gretta said. Christmas World is in trouble?"

Bruno nodded. "Since my father retired, visitor numbers and satisfaction have been plummeting a little more each year. Eventually, I don't think they'll be anything left of it," he admitted glumly.

She looked to where Gretta had disappeared to. The woman was still behind closed doors in the back.

It made Hannah feel she could ask her next question without reserve. "Do you mean the resort is in danger of closing?"

He sighed heavily. "It was a mistake allowing anyone but my family to take care of this place. My great-grandfather founded Christmas World you know. He wanted a place where it could be Christmas every day."

A soft chuckle left his lips, and Hannah found herself smiling as she listened to him.

"You ever realize how everything seems brighter and better at Christmas?" His light green eyes lit up as he spoke. "It's as if nothing bad could happen. My great-grandfather wanted to try and keep that feeling all year round. What better way than to create a place where it really could be Christmas every day?"

"This place is like this all the time?" Hannah was incredulous. She thought the resort was just for the holiday season.

"Not any more, but it used to be," Bruno replied, his eyes shifting away from her.

She truly didn't know what to say. Yes, initially she felt as if she'd been almost tricked into coming to Christmas World, and that the place closing was surely better than letting it keep going the way it was.

But that was before she'd met Bruno. He wasn't some manipulative, money-hungry capitalist exploiting people's hard-earned money and expectations.

He was a former soldier - a man who'd fought for their country - who'd taken over a family business after illness and after poor management had almost run it into the ground.

"You could change things, you know," she murmured.

His eyes snapped up to meet hers.

"You could," Hannah insisted more forcefully. She flashed him an encouraging smile. He cared about his family legacy. That was more than enough motivation to turn things around.

"Thanks for saying that. But I don't think so."

"I mean it," she insisted. "You can improve things. Turn this place around."

"You sound like my Dad."

"Then he's a very smart man," Hannah mused. She sipped at her hot chocolate. It was superb. It was so good she hadn't even yet considered what was on the menu.

"Yes, he is," Bruno answered. "The smartest man I know. It's just he can't take the pressure associated with the business anymore."

"Making one person happy is sometimes impossible, so I can't imagine making hundreds of them happy would be a walk in the park," she commented. "However, with even just a few small changes, things could be different. Get rid of the awful lighting for a start. And introduce some evening activities to entertain the visitors. There needs to be something to occupy them in the darkness too. Also, why does the kitchen at the lodge close so early? The chef leaves well before people get a chance to get good and hungry. And local flair," she added, warming to her theme. "You need artisans for specialty items only found here in these parts, not that carbon-copy plastic junk that's on sale now."

Hannah could have slapped her hand over her mouth, but that would have been even more humiliating than her endless chatter.

Her tangents were going to get her into trouble if she didn't rein them in.

"Sorry," she said then. "Sometimes my tongue thinks it knows everything, and my brain is slow to catch up and tell it to shut up," she commented. She wanted to crawl under the table.

"No, keep going," Bruno said. He was leaning forward in his seat listening intently. "I think you have something there. Restoring the old lighting system *would* make things cheerier, and the artisans could give visitors something unique to remember us by. Maybe even something like a collection, so they get a new piece from here every time they visit?"

"Exactly!" Hannah smiled as a tingle of excitement rushed through her.

She loved all things Christmas, possibly because she'd never experienced the traditional picture postcard kind, and planning for the holidays was one of her favorite things to do.

"I like the idea of more activities in the evening. Things to keep guests entertained and even bring people together," Bruno continued, and Hannah could almost see the cogs in his mind turning now. "Maybe a show or something?"

"Absolutely." She sipped again at her chocolate. "I told you that you could turn this place around. Just doing those few things would make a huge improvement. More like what people expect when they come here." Then she laughed. "I should probably just make you a list."

The door to the back room of the café opened then, and Gretta came out. "You two ready to order?"

Hannah smiled at Bruno, who smiled back. "Not quite yet, Gretta, we actually got a bit lost in conversation," he chuckled. "Give us a couple more minutes?"

She nodded with a knowing smile. "Sure. Just holler and I'll come back out."

Hannah pulled the menu to her. "We better pick something though. I'm sure Gretta wants to close this place up."

"Nah," Bruno dismissed with a shrug. "She'd stay open all night as long as there's someone here. She likes the company. Usually, she's here alone testing recipes and prepping for the next day."

Hannah looked again at the door to the back. "Alone?"

"Yes. She doesn't have any family. Her son moved to Anchorage earlier this year. Things weren't going so well with the lull in visitors here, so he moved to help his family."

"Which means changing things around would do so much for the locals here too," she mused. "Make so many people's lives very different."

"You know ... you say it like a joke, but I really think you should."

Hannah's eyes darted up. "Should what?"

"Make a list. I mean, I have to admit - I'm really no good with this stuff. I've lived here all my life, so I have no real idea what visitors expect. No idea how to create the fairytale Christmas experience people want. That *you* expected. So tell me."

Hannah sat back in her chair. She wanted to help him, but could her suggestions really make a difference? It's not as though she was any kind of expert in event planning or business; she was a photographer for goodness sake....

Then remembering, she looked balefully at her injured arm. "Well, it's not as though I have anything better to do ..." she grimaced.

"And in exchange, I'll help *you* complete your assignment," Bruno told her, his eyes lighting up suddenly. "Let *me* be your right arm, maybe help you get those photos you need?" he continued, enthused afresh. "You can show me exactly what to do, and I can take the shots for you. That way we *both* win. I help you get the pictures you need for your assignment, and you help me turn this place around."

"I - "

"I know where to find the auroras," he blurted then, and Hannah's eyes widened.

"You do?"

"Of course. I've lived here my entire life, remember? Spent much of my childhood chasing the lights. I can take you to the best vantage points, and if you show me what to do, I can also make sure you get the best pictures for your work. You can still get the job done, and help out a community of struggling people at the same time. What do you say?"

Hannah's heart raced a little. It was a very interesting proposition.

She could still visualize her name under the shots in *Discover Wild,* maybe even a short editorial about her. The prospects it could mean for her career.

She bit her lip. *Could they really pull this off?*

"The best places?" she repeated.

Bruno smiled. "The very best."

"Alright. You have a deal. You make sure I get the most amazing pictures of the Northern Lights that anyone has ever seen, and I'll do my best to help you turn the tables on this town and put the magic back into Christmas World. Agreed?"

She extended her good hand toward him.

Bruno took it, and they shook firmly.

"Deal."

CHAPTER 16

She could already see the change in Bruno's eyes. It was as if she'd just shot him full of hope.

Their gazes remained on one another for several moments and Hannah felt her heart beat just a tad faster. She needed to do something before the silence made it explode.

"Um … we better get something to eat," she muttered. "We have a lot of planning to do. That's always best on a full stomach."

"Good point."

Hannah looked over the menu while Bruno gave some suggestions on what to choose. She truly hoped she *could* help him now, though she wasn't sure how much they could really achieve in the short term.

But at least they could try.

BREAKFAST FOR DINNER was highly underrated, but Hannah was a big fan. She plucked two fluffy pancakes from the serving plate and topped them with warm maple syrup, whipped cream, and fresh strawberries. Then added some strips of crispy bacon, three sausage links and hash browns.

"I like that," Bruno said smiling.

She looked up at him with a mouthful of pancake, then chewed it quickly and swallowed. "What?"

"A woman with a good appetite."

Hannah snorted as she laughed. "Yeah, I do like to eat." She enjoyed another mouthful. "I don't see the point in starving yourself. Your body needs food to fuel it, so you might as well enjoy it."

"I like the way you think. Sometimes I feel we overthink things in this world. Make it complicated just for the sake of it, as if it gives us some control."

"Life is short," Hannah replied. "And has so much to offer that we miss out worrying about stuff that's just trivial in the grand scheme, chasing things we don't care about because we have bills to pay. Starve ourselves of some really great food because we're worried about what we look like to people who don't even notice." She took another bite. "Don't get me wrong, of course you should aim to be healthy, but you don't need to starve yourself or eat boring food to do that."

"You sound like a spokeswoman for Jenny Craig or something," Bruno mused.

She chuckled. "No, just some of my late dad's wisdom."

"Another wise man?"

"Yep" she answered. "A very wise man. OK, so I guess I'll need to teach you the basics of using a camera."

"Don't you just point and shoot?"

She looked at him in dismay. "Tell me you're kidding."

"I'm kidding," he chuckled. "I know there's a lot more to it than that. There's a reason why we aren't all working for magazines."

Not everyone understood photography. They thought it was simple. You just magically found the perfect setting and took the shot.

But it took much more than that. It took timing, lighting, the right angle and ... the perfect moment.

It wasn't something that just happened either. Sometimes you had to make it happen.

"We can work on that tomorrow, but for now let's make a start on *my* part of the bargain. And the first thing that needs to change in Christmas World is those tacky fluorescents," she scolded playfully. "They need to go - like, yesterday."

"Consider them gone," Bruno declared with a grin.

"Then we need to do something to improve the spirit of this place. It's supposed to be festive and cheery, but your elves are anything but. I don't think I've ever seen a more glum bunch in my entire life."

Bruno chuckled. "Cheer up the elves. Got it."

"And Santa too," she added, warming to her theme. "That guy *seriously* needs a makeover."

CHAPTER 17

The following days seemed to pass in a blur as Hannah and Bruno made plans and changes.

It was strange, but having improvements as her focus immediately helped brighten up the place's former atmosphere.

Suddenly, Christmas World had endless potential, and she, Hannah, was a part of it.

"How are things coming with the new lighting?" she asked, as she and Bruno ambled down a snowy main street together, while nearby, workmen were dismantling the overhead lights.

"The electrician promised me that everything will be good to go in time for tonight's s'mores roast," he informed. "We should have everything right on schedule."

"Excellent. That really will be the perfect thing to get the Christmas spirit flowing around here."

"The snowball throw isn't enough?" Bruno queried, chuckling.

The idea for a guest snowball throw involving locals and

visitors had come to her a day after their impromptu dinner at Gretta's.

It was one of those cool wintery activities Hannah had always wanted to do; that, and make snow angels.

If she liked it she was sure others would too, and such an inclusive public event seemed the perfect way to mark the beginning of the big Christmas World turnaround.

In the meantime, Bruno had designed colorful fliers to announce some of the other festive happenings after they'd got the staff on board.

When they'd met with the staff Hannah had initially expected some protests, but she was surprised to find that they quite liked the boss's new ideas.

It got some of the staff members talking about their own favorite Christmas activities, which in turn, gave Bruno even more inspiration and incentive to transform the place once and for all.

Today was a light snow day. Hannah's hair was pulled into a high ponytail atop her head, and she was wearing a slightly lighter jacket now that she had grown more accustomed to the cold.

"Should we head over to the forest? It's almost time." She strolled beside Bruno with her camera slung over her shoulder.

Her wrist wasn't hurting as much as the first day; the medication from Dr. Morgan had helped a lot, as did the exercises.

She was supposed to wait a little bit longer before she used it, but was still impatient to get back to her photography.

"You want me to take that?" He reached for the camera strap.

"Thanks."

"Don't mention it," he replied. "After all, I'm the one who's supposed to be taking over. I figure this will be a good learning exercise."

"Yep," Hannah smiled. "Let's see what you can do."

THE WOODS AREA to the west of the town had been transformed for tonight's first Christmas World Snowball Throw.

Mounds of pre-rolled snowballs were dotted between the trees.

It was one of the more fun tasks the staff had to do in years. Hannah couldn't join in to help, but had overseen the work and the positioning of the stacks earlier that afternoon.

Guests, staff and some locals were already gathered. They all stood around, not quite sure what do to, as she and Bruno approached.

She turned to him. "You're on, Mr. CEO."

He smiled nervously.

"You got this," Hannah whispered, patting his arm encouragingly. "Go get 'em."

She watched as Bruno walked into the midst of the gathered crowd. He raised a hand in greeting as he began to speak, and despite his smile, she knew he was inwardly terrified.

"Hey everyone, welcome to the inaugural Christmas World Snowball Throw. This year, we wanted to offer our visitors something new to do in our holiday town. We're changing it up and shaking things up, to ensure that you have the most memorable Christmas of your life."

The applause was small, but there were smiles on the faces of those gathered.

Hannah was sure some were a little skeptical of what was happening. People didn't often take sudden changes well, but in this case, it was all for the best.

This is going to work. I know it will.

CHAPTER 18

Hannah smiled as Bruno then sounded the charge for the fun to begin.

The moment the words were out of his mouth, elated screams and snowballs began to fly through the air in every direction.

She had to duck behind a tree to avoid getting caught in the crossfire and laughed as Bruno approached her, already covered in snow.

He'd gotten in a few early throws and some of his staff had returned the favor before he'd been able to make his retreat.

"What'd you think? A good start?" he laughed as he shook the snow from his golden hair.

"I'll say. Better get that camera ready," she replied. "You're also tonight's event photographer."

"Right." He took the Nikon from her and removed the lens cap.

"First, hold it up and get a feel for it. Then take a few candid shots."

"Of what?"

"Whatever you like, or whoever. I wanna see what kind of eye you have," she stated.

He looked at her with a cocked brow. "Alright. I'll give it a try." He turned to the volleys of snowballs and began snapping away.

At first, he didn't move around much, but as he got more into it his feet began to shift, he started adjusting the position of the camera in his hands, and she could see he was getting lost in the moment, zoning in on various groups of snowballers as they laughed and enjoyed themselves.

Hannah smiled. That was what she'd hoped for.

If Bruno could get comfortable with the camera on his own terms, not just taking direction from her, it would mean all the difference once they really got going.

Photography needed heart.

I can't give him mine, but I can at least try to tease out his.

She continued to watch him. The happier and more confident he became with the shots he was taking, the more optimistic she felt.

BY THE TIME the snowball throw was over and it was time for the s'mores roast, she could tell that Bruno was really enjoying himself.

Now, the gaudy fluorescent lighting was gone, and strings of pretty white fairylights were draped on lampposts all the way round the town square. It looked magical.

Barbecue pits and s'mores stations had been established for visitors to gather their ingredients before taking everything to campfire pits and gather round.

Hannah took her camera back from Bruno as he collected food for them both.

In the meantime, she did her best to use one hand and take a few shots herself. They weren't great; they weren't even good, but still, they were something to capture the moment.

Tonight, for the first time since she'd got here, people in Christmas World looked cheery and festive, and more importantly, everyone was smiling.

It was the exactly the kind of atmosphere Hannah had been expecting, the kind of memorable moment she'd been hoping for when she first came here.

Then another idea struck her, and her eyes widened.

"What is it?" Bruno questioned as he returned to her with a teetering pile of marshmallows and chocolate.

"I've just thought of something; another improvement. How about a photo contest? Your most memorable Christmas World moment. Give everyone here the impetus to capture some fun moments for themselves while here … and they could also maybe win a prize of some sort? Entries could be posted on the notice board at Santa's Post Office and a winner announced at the end of every week."

"Where do you come up with these ideas? They're brilliant," he chuckled.

She grinned happily. "Hey I'm a photographer, remember? Capturing magic moments is what I do. And making them happen is what *you* do, or will be from now on," she teased.

"You know, I think you deserve something more than just a roasted s'more," Bruno mused. "You have so many great ideas I can't keep up with them."

"Well, if you're offering, then maybe one of Gretta's legendary hot chocolates later?"

"I'll take you there after this."

"It's a date."

The words hung in the air, as he stared at her.

Oh your stupid mouth again, Hannah.

She laughed nervously. "You know what I meant. Not a date-date, just a…"

"No need to explain," Bruno replied, his expression unreadable but his eyes were twinkling. "Hot chocolate it is."

CHAPTER 19

In the days that followed, Christmas World began to become truly alive with the spirit of the season.

The change in mood was remarkable, so much so that it even drew Bruno's father back out into the holiday resort town he'd managed for most of his life.

Gerald Locke was slightly overweight with square-framed glasses and a salt-and-pepper beard that ran from his temples down his jaw and merged with his thick mustache.

His face was round and his hair was trimmed close to his head. He had a brilliant, jolly smile that made Hannah think of her dad when she saw him, even though they looked nothing alike.

And Santa of course.

"Evening, Mr Locke," Hannah greeted as she walked up to him in Gretta's.

He was at the same table where she and Bruno had come up with the idea to save Christmas World, and since that day they'd done most of their planning there.

Gretta seemed to love it, plus the increased clientele now

coming through. Evening opening hours everywhere in the town had been extended, and once the visitors knew that, they came out in droves.

Though it didn't matter how busy the café was, Gretta made sure Hannah and Bruno's window table was always available for them.

"Hannah," the old man grumbled good-naturedly. "How many times must I tell you to call me Gerald?"

She smiled as she pulled out the seat beside him and lowered herself onto the chair.

"OK then, Gerald," she corrected. "You're looking great today."

"I feel great. It's nice to be out of retirement," he commented jokingly.

When Bruno had presented to the old Santa the idea of doing a full reindeer-led sleigh ride through town on Christmas Eve to distribute gifts to everyone, the current incumbent was immediately adamant that he wasn't going to do it.

He didn't like reindeer. He didn't like sleighs. He didn't like having to cry 'Ho-ho-ho' either.

Hannah couldn't fathom why the guy even had the job of being Santa in the first place. However, when Gerald had heard their plans, he immediately wanted to be a part of it.

Bruno had very quickly shared their ideas with his dad, and Mr Locke Senior had wanted to meet the woman who'd triggered all of these new changes.

Initially, Hannah had been nervous about meeting Bruno's dad, but at the same time, she was curious.

And was very pleasantly surprised.

The Locke men were the funniest when put together.

They were constantly teasing one another, rehashing old stories and laughing.

Dinner at Bruno's house was one of the most memorable evenings she'd had in a long time, and as all three talked about various other plans for Christmas World, Hannah found that she was liking the project more than she'd expected.

Initially, it had been a response to the obvious shortcomings of the holiday resort, but as she and Bruno had gotten further into the planning, and she could see how even the simplest changes were beginning to transform not only the town, but the people in it, it began to mean so much more.

It began to truly reflect what Christmas was about – community and togetherness.

It was also somewhat of a revelation for Hannah, who was used to remaining behind the lens, as opposed to being part of a scene.

She was so accustomed to experiencing things from afar, that it was actually somewhat overwhelming to now be right in the heart of all the excitement and fun.

And she was liking that bit far more than she'd anticipated.

Now, the door of the café opened and Bruno walked in.

A huge smile spread across Hannah's face at the sight of him.

It was completely involuntary, but the second she saw him it was like getting that Christmas gift you always wanted.

Stop it. Don't be silly. This is business.

She turned to find Gerald staring at her. "I think your assistant is here," he commented, biting into a cookie.

"Should you be eating that?" she chided.

"I'm getting into my role," Gerald replied. "What's a Santa who doesn't eat cookies?"

"Thinner," his son finished deadpan, and Hannah chuckled. Bruno turned to her. "Ready to go?"

"Got everything right here." She raised her camera bag.

"Perfect." He stepped around her chair and collected both her haversack and her camera bag from the floor beside her, before tossing both over his shoulders. "Time to shoot for the stars."

CHAPTER 20

Most of all, Hannah loved their nights beneath the sky.

Bruno really had been true to his word; he knew all the best vantage points for the Northern Lights, and now he sat beside her on the sled as they stared in awe at the radiating colors.

"Every night really is different," she commented breathlessly, as bands of ethereal green danced in the sky above them.

"I know," Bruno smiled. "That's what's great about it. You never know what to expect."

"Could you imagine seeing this every day?"

Bruno's pale green eyes seemed to radiate with a light of their own under the magnetic rays. "Yes, because I do."

Hannah laughed as she looked back at him. "Of course."

"Having someone to share it with makes it different, though," he added gently. "I'm glad you're here."

"So am I."

Her heart fluttered.

Stop it, Hannah. It's not like that. He's just holding up his part of the deal.

Every day she had to remind herself that what was between her and Bruno was purely business.

However, the more time she spent with him alone, together beneath the stars, the more difficult it was for her to come to terms about that fact.

She looked back up at the sky. "So now, get the shot in frame …" she instructed.

Bruno duly manoeuvred the camera lens back up and began to take more photos.

It was the best way to distract herself.

The more Hannah focused on work, the less she could think of Bruno Locke or the way his eyes made her want to look into them every single day. Nor the stir of her heart when she did.

He set the camera aside again after a few minutes.

"Pass me the coffee from my bag?" He leaned over to fetch the rucksack himself, having realized it was on the same side as her bad arm.

In the meantime, Hannah had reached across to grab the flask with her good hand, and turned back, only to meet him midway.

Their noses practically touched, and her breath caught at their proximity. Her gaze met his and she thought Bruno seemed as affected by their closeness as she did, but for some reason, neither of them moved.

They just stayed there, staring into each other's eyes.

Hannah's heart began to dance in her chest as her breath quickened.

"Bruno?" she whispered, after what felt like forever.

"Yes?"

"Here's your coffee."

She watched him swallow the lump in his throat, and he blinked several times before sitting back as he reached for the flask. "Thanks."

"You're welcome."

"Maybe we should head back soon," he suggested as he set the flask aside unopened. "It's getting late."

"Good idea," she replied distractedly, still a little discombobulated.

What was happening? It felt as if her skin was magnetized, it was tingling so much and her heart still hadn't calmed.

He got to his feet first, and helped her up after him, before starting to pack up the equipment.

Hannah wanted to help, but he insisted that she should just get herself comfortable on the sled for the journey back, and she duly began to move some stuff to make more room.

Bruno's rucksack was still open, so she went to zip it back up, until something inside caught her eye.

Some words on a white page inside.

Her curiosity piqued, she looked back to where he was still packing up their stuff, before pulling the document out further, scanning it quickly.

It was a property sale agreement ... For Christmas World.

Hannah's galloping heart stopped for a moment as her eyes moved to the bottom of the page.

Signed and dated by Bruno.

CHAPTER 21

Hannah could hardly look at him since, she felt so betrayed.

He'd made her believe he wanted to turn things around for Christmas World, but he'd already signed the documents to sell it.

Why was he wasting her time - and everyone else's?

She felt like a fraud walking amongst the resort staff now, seeing their optimistic faces and hearing their excited chatter about all of the changes so far.

Knowing that it was all a lie. Their boss was a liar and even worse, she was his accomplice.

It isn't your business, Hannah.

Christmas World is Bruno's and if he wants to sell it what does it have to do with you?

He can do whatever he wants. So what if he used you to make things better. He probably just made those improvements to make the place more attractive to buyers.

You were just too blinded by charisma and good-looks to notice. You should know better.

Things aren't always what they seem.

Now at the lodge, Hannah sat on the edge of her bed and mulled over the discovery that had been plaguing her ever since she'd happened across the truth.

Should she just leave now without saying anything, or should she confront him?

She picked up her scarf and wrapped it around her neck. Bruno and Gerald were expecting her at the café today.

They were seated at their usual table, but Hannah didn't have the same warm feeling she'd grown accustomed to at seeing them.

Now she looked at Bruno and felt only disappointment.

At both him and herself.

But for his dad's sake, she did her best to hide it.

"Hannah, Dad and I were just talking about the photo competition. Submissions finished today, so now we just need to check the entries and declare a winner. I was thinking you and I could do that after Gretta closes up for the day? Everything else is pretty much all set up and ready for the Big Night," Bruno added, referring to the upcoming Santa Departure celebrations; the culmination of all the changes they'd already made.

He was grinning like the cat that swallowed the canary.

"Oh," she replied. "About that," she began. "I won't actually be here for the Christmas Eve party after all."

"Why not, Hannah?" Gerald asked, concerned. "Has something happened?"

"I've just decided that it's high time I got home."

"But I thought you were going to stay on till after Christmas?" Bruno questioned. "After all the hard work you put in, surely you'd want to be here to celebrate with everyone. The pinnacle of all your wonderful ideas. You can't miss that, Hannah. I mean, what about..." Then he trailed off, as if about to say something else, but thinking better of it.

She glared at him. How could he talk about celebrating, given what he was planning to do as soon as everything was over?

Were the new buyers going to be there on Christmas Eve? Would they be coming out just to see how 'special' the place could be?

Then she thought of something else. Had Bruno signed the deal with them before or after he'd dazzled Hannah with the aurora borealis?

"I don't have to be there. This is for the people who belong here."

"But it wouldn't be anything without you," Gerald countered. "You made it all possible."

She forced a smile. "Thank you, Gerald, but I'm sure Bruno would have come up with something on his own. I just gave him a nudge in the right direction."

"It was more than a nudge," he protested. "You inspired all of this - everything."

Hannah felt her eyes sting. *Don't remind me.*

"Hey, there is something wrong," Bruno pressed. He was looking at her keenly and she did everything she could to avoid his gaze.

"Bruno," his dad said calmly. "If Hannah needs to go she needs to go." Gerald smiled at her. "We were very lucky to have her and her ideas to help us out," he continued. "But we can't keep her forever, and she has her own life back in California."

Hannah swallowed in an attempt to clear the thickening in her throat.

"That's right. I've got everything I needed for my assignment. Now, I need to go home."

Bruno pushed away from the table and got to his feet. "Excuse me."

She watched as he left the café without another word.

He's acting hurt, but it's not his emotion to feel.

He's the one who lied. The one who tricked, who betrayed everyone.

Hannah folded her arms over her chest.

She couldn't wait to get on that plane and home to reality.

Things weren't so magical anymore in Christmas World.

CHAPTER 22

❄

She stayed on with Gerald in the cafe for a bit while they had lunch together. If Bruno wanted to sulk or get upset it was his business.

It had nothing to do with her.

Nothing here has anything to do with me. I came for a job. I got my photos, that's all I came for.

Nothing more.

It was later when Bruno returned with the photo competition entry box. The café was by then quieter and Gretta was out back preparing for the evening trade.

The older woman had since confided that things had turned around so much that if it continued, her son might even be able to leave his job in Anchorage and come back home.

Hannah hoped she wouldn't be disappointed. Who knew what the new owners would do with the place once they took over?

"Will you help with these before you go?" Bruno asked her

tersely, as he put the box on the table between her and Gerald. "It's kind of your speciality after all."

She barely looked at him. "Sure."

There were dozens of entries, and as the three sorted through all the happy Christmas World memories captured by families and couples over the last week or so, Hannah felt even more disheartened.

"So much to choose from," she mused. "How can we possibly pick a winner?"

"Well, *I* think it's obvious," Gerald smiled, staring at the photograph he was holding.

He looked over at Bruno. "Yours wins hands down, son."

"What?" Hannah asked, surprised. "Bruno entered a photo?"

He looked at her sheepishly. "I did," he replied. "I wanted it to be a surprise."

"And you think it should win?" she asked Gerald in disbelief. OK, so she'd taught Bruno a lot about photography, but she couldn't see how it could be *that* good.

Then Gerald slid the picture in her direction and Hannah stared in disbelief.

It was a candid shot of her beneath the night sky; her face illuminated by the Northern Lights as she stared in awe at the spectacle.

The pure wonder in her expression was deeply vivid, so much so that at the time, Hannah never even realized that Bruno had turned the lens on her.

She was shocked to see how well he'd captured the emotion she was feeling just then. He made her look ... radiant. The way any photographer who truly cared about his subject might.

Now, her gaze rose to meet Bruno's. How could he take a picture like that and lie to her all this time?

How could the photo suggest the kind of affection and respect that the things he'd done belied?

What was real?

"I ... have to go," she muttered, suddenly.

Hannah rushed out of the café, unable to say any more. She slipped her arms into her jacket, but didn't let the action slow her pace. She needed to get as far away from Bruno (and that picture) as possible.

"Hannah," a voice called out from behind her then.

She turned to find his dad struggling to catch up in the snow and she slowed immediately. "Gerald?"

"Thank you for stopping," the older man said. "I was afraid I'd have to run after you to catch up. You'd be back at the lodge by the time I managed it," he chuckled.

"I wouldn't run away from you," she said fondly.

"I know," he replied. "What I don't know is why you're running at all."

Her expression was guarded. "What do you mean?"

"You raced out of there as if wild dogs were after you," he mused. "Something's going on Hannah. I want to know what's wrong."

She shook her head. "It's nothing. I just need to go home."

He looked at her. "You know, don't you?"

"Know what?"

"About the sale," he stated and Hannah's heart dropped to her toes.

"You know about that?" she asked, incredulously.

Gerald's gaze fell for a moment. "Of course. Bruno signed the contract a couple of weeks ago, but I asked him for one last Christmas to see if things turned around before I cosigned," he admitted. "He can't sign away Christmas World without me, you see."

Then he met her eyes and smiled. "I hoped something would happen to change things - a Christmas miracle of sorts. And I was right," he continued happily. "You appeared. You inspired my son and look at what's happened!" He gestured around the enlivened town square. "Bruno finally has a vision for this place - his vision, not mine or my father's or grandfather's. You gave him confidence to keep our legacy going. *You* were the change we all so badly needed." He plucked her chin lightly, while she tried to get to grips with what she was hearing. "Hannah, you were exactly the little piece of Christmas magic I was holding out for."

CHAPTER 23

*H*annah couldn't move. She could hardly think.

What was Gerald saying? Were they selling Christmas World or not?

"I assure you, Bruno has no intention of selling this place now," the older man confirmed. "Neither do I. This Christmas will be the best we've had here in a long time, and I anticipate many more to come."

"And we have you to thank for that, Hannah," Bruno interrupted gently.

She hadn't noticed him approach, but now he was standing a few feet away from them.

Gerald turned to his son and smiled. "I think I can leave you to explain the rest," he stated, then turned and began to shuffle slowly back toward the café.

Hannah remained motionless. She'd spent the past couple of days slowly growing to resent Bruno, but now she was hearing that she was wrong about him, about everything.

She still wasn't sure she believed it, though.

"Hannah," he began, as he took slow steps toward her, the

way she herself approached wildlife to photograph, so as not to frighten them into running.

Was that what Bruno felt? Was he afraid she'd run away?

Her heart was racing. She watched as he grew closer and part of her wanted to leave, but another part needed to stay and hear him out.

She wanted to be wrong about what she'd come to believe. She wanted there to be more than what she was telling herself.

"I didn't want to tell you about the sale," Bruno stated gently. "Or admit that I'd given up on this place long before I met you. I was just holding on for my dad's sake, hoping to get through this one last season before we gave it all up for good." He stepped closer. "I didn't have a vision before. I didn't believe I could turn things around. I didn't even know how."

Hannah swallowed her galloping heart.

"I thought selling was the best thing to do. It would allow Dad to have an easy life, no stress from running this place and enough money to take care of his retirement." Bruno sighed. "Better than running our family's legacy into the ground. Then I met you," he continued, taking a final step toward her. "And everything changed. You changed everything - for me."

"Bruno…"

"When I saw Christmas World through your eyes, Hannah, it opened mine," he continued, undeterred. "Your disappointment and your vision, it helped me to see that this wasn't just about business - it was about the people who come here to have a magical, once in a lifetime festive experience. It wasn't even about the family legacy, it was about what my great-grandfather originally wanted, a place where people could experience the real joy of Christmas."

"That's really great, Bruno. I'm glad you found your way. I

told you that you would," she replied guardedly. "But what does it have to do with me?"

"Everything," he insisted reaching for her good hand. "It means everything."

Hannah searched his eyes as he continued to speak. Her ears could hardly believe what she was hearing.

Bruno's thumbs caressed the back of her wrist and her heart danced at the sensation.

This his hand released hers and rose to her cheek, until he held her face gently. "Do you know why I took that picture, Hannah?"

"No," she whispered. "I don't even know *when* you took it."

He smiled. "You were so lost in the auroras, in that magic they create that you didn't notice when I turned the camera away from the lights to you. I had to capture you, to hold on to you - and that moment. I didn't know if I'd ever get another chance, so I took it."

"Another chance to do what?" Hannah asked.

She was shocked that the words were even able to come out of her mouth. Her tongue seemed to have stopped working somewhere along the way from when Bruno started to talk until this moment.

He stifled a laugh. "You had me the first day I met you, did you know that?"

She shook her head.

"The moment I saw you standing there in the snow waving at me, calling out. Then, even when you started grumbling about Christmas World, I realized you were someone I wanted to know better," he continued. "The more I got to know, the more I wanted to know, and the more I didn't want you to leave. But I knew I couldn't keep you here either. I knew you were here for a reason, and once that was over you'd leave - so I had to hold on to what I could. Immortalize how I felt, I guess."

She thought her heart was going to crash out of her chest it was beating so loudly against her ribs.

Hannah sucked in a deep breath. "I thought I was the only one who was feeling that," she whispered. "I tried to pretend I didn't."

Bruno's hands slid down the side of her neck and settled on her shoulders.

"I couldn't hide it any longer," he stated as his arms closed gently around her and he pulled her closer. "I tried. I really did. I wanted to pretend I didn't feel the way I do, but I can't deny it, Hannah. That's why I entered the picture in the competition. I couldn't tell you how I felt, so I thought that … maybe I could *show* you. Especially after our last night out there, beneath the stars." He smiled. "I really wanted to kiss you then, you know."

"Why didn't you?" she asked but her throat was so dry she could hardly hear her own voice.

There was no fighting the irresistible tug between them and Hannah didn't need to, not when she knew Bruno felt the same for her as she did for him.

"Because I didn't know if you'd want me to. Hannah, you don't know how much I struggled not to when you were so close. All I had to do was lean forward an inch and touch your lips with mine …"

She allowed herself to melt into him, losing all thought of anything else as she savored the warmth of his breath amidst the cold night air.

"… like this."

Before finally, Bruno's lips met hers.

CHAPTER 24

❄

*L*ater, the two of them stood again out on the tundra, watching another truly spectacular aurora display.

Shimmering green zigzagged through the sky in wondrous illumination, as Hannah stood wrapped in the warmth of Bruno's arms.

"So have you decided then?" he whispered in her ear from behind. His lips caressed her earlobe as he spoke, and she felt a tingle run up her spine.

"Decided what?" she replied nonchalantly.

He chuckled. "You know," he asked nuzzling at her cheek. "What's it going to be? Will you stay here for Christmas and enjoy the changes you've wrought to this town, and my life, or are you going to disappear back to California and forget all about us?"

Hannah's heart stuttered. She took a deep breath and turned to face him.

"I came here with one mission – get great shots of the aurora borealis, and the job of my dreams. But to be honest, being forced to step away from the lens for a while kind of made me realize how much I hide away from being a part of what's going on around me."

He looked confused. "But you travel all over with your photography. You're constantly in the middle of things."

"Not really," she explained. "Yes, I go out looking for the perfect picture. But I never let myself be in it. Here, I got the chance to step out from behind the camera and be part of the scene, as it were."

Bruno smiled, pulling her even closer. He smelled of aftershave, dark chocolate and mint. She rested her head on his chest.

"Well, clearly you are talented on both sides. We already have repeat bookings for next year, and some of the artisans have even approached me about getting their store space back once I reduced the prices."

Hannah looked up at him. "I told you, you could do it."

"Only because I had you to help me. I don't know if I really could've done it without you."

"Of course you could."

"No," he countered. "I mean it. You made all the difference." He gazed into her eyes. "Anyway I'm not sure I'd *want* to do it without you," he continued.

She looked at him. "What do you mean?"

He ran his fingers through his hair. "I know I should give you time, but I'm saying straight out, that I don't want you to go, Hannah," Bruno answered. "I'm saying that I've fallen for you and I'd love the chance to see if maybe there's something more here than just a Christmas romance ..."

She wasn't breathing. She couldn't breathe. It was crazy. They barely knew each other.

But then why was she smiling so much?

"Bruno, this is very sudden," she replied as she tried to catch her breath.

"I know. But I'm just telling you that I know how *I* feel. I don't play games, Hannah. I'm not built that way," he continued. "I believe there's more than a chance for us, but I can't do it alone. I know you'll get the job with the magazine, but how about shooting for the stars with me?"

She smiled, not so confident about her prospects with *Discover Wild* but even if she did get the job, as a freelancer, she could still work from anywhere.

"So let me get this straight, you're offering me the chance to stay in a snow-filled winter wonderland where it's Christmas every day, and every night you get to watch the world's most magical natural phenomenon beneath a starlit sky... every photographer's dream."

He was grinning from ear-to-ear. "So does that mean...?"

Hannah closed her eyes and lost herself in the moment, one she suspected would be the first of many.

She'd come here for an assignment but was staying for love, not just for Bruno, but to be part of a place that truly did make dreams come true and opened up magical possibilities in the everyday.

Here, she could experience that wonder all the time, plus a chance at the kind of happiness she'd never known.

"I'm staying," she told him, smiling as he kissed her. "For Christmas, and as long as you'll have me."

12 DOGS OF CHRISTMAS

❄

A FESTIVE HOLIDAY TAIL

CHAPTER 1

The curtains were wide open when Lucy Adams woke up. She must have forgotten to close them the night before, and now she was glad for that.

Snow outlined the windowsill like a frame, and the blanketed San Juan Mountains - the sun just peeking above its summit - was the picture.

It was a beautiful sight to wake up to.

She sighed happily. Small town life was very different to what it had been like in Denver, but she should have known the city wasn't for her.

Lucy was a Whitedale native, born and bred.

Once upon a time, she thought that time in the big city would help her shyness, and allow her to live out her grandmother's dream of her becoming a success.

Gran had been so sure that Lucy becoming an investigative journalist and seeing her name on the by-line of a story would have spurred her on to even greater things, but it didn't.

Because she never got any further than being a fact checker.

Lucy was cripplingly shy; always had been. When she was a child her mother tried everything to help bring her out of her shell, but it was no use.

Her timidity and innate reserve around people made it difficult for her to even broach the subject of an article to her boss.

In the end, she realized that no matter how hard she tried, she'd never be as happy in Denver as she would be back home.

So home she came.

Now, she swung her legs from beneath the sheets and did a few quick stretches to loosen herself up for the day ahead. Then quickly made her bed; the wrinkled sheets and pillow depressed on only one side.

Her apartment was the best she could afford; a small upper-level two-bed on Maypole Avenue, close to all the parks and trails.

When she started renting it a couple of years ago, she'd sort of hoped that by now she'd have someone to share it with, but no such luck.

Lucy didn't know why, but she seemed to have been born without the romance gene too.

She knew she wasn't bad looking, with her shoulder-length caramel-colored hair and fair skin. Her smile was big and warm, but the problem likely was that she didn't really smile around people.

Animals yes; humans not so much.

People made her nervous, which was why having a dog-walking business was a plus. Lucy spent her days surrounded entirely by those who understood her without judgment.

Lucy was very proud of her business, 12 Dogs Walking

Service. It was the premier dog-walking outfit in town, and she had dreams of making it even better.

Once she had enough money saved and found the right location, she fully intended to add other services, like doggie daycare and pet pampering.

She envisioned her little business as one day being the best animal care center in the county, if not the state.

But hey, one day at a time.

THE WOODEN FLOORS were cool beneath her feet as Lucy left her bedroom and walked into the kitchen.

She fixed herself a bowl of cereal and a cup of coffee while waiting for her computer to wake.

She loved her trusty old-model Dell PC, but Betsy was on her last legs. It used to take less than a minute for it to boot up, now it was more like seven.

Lucy hummed the lyrics to *Must Have Been the Mistletoe* as she got out her apple cinnamon granola and almond milk. She did her best to eat well, and in Whitedale that was made easier by the popularity of the farm-to-table movement.

Then she settled at her two-seater dining table by the small window overlooking the square.

The town was slowly coming to life - in a few hours, cars and people would be bustling along the streets, but for the moment it was just store owners looking for an early start, and a few joggers out for a morning run.

When the PC was fully loaded, the home screen flickered to life, and a picture of a golden-haired cocker spaniel greeted Lucy, making her smile immediately.

"So let's see what's going on today…" she mumbled as she opened her emails; a couple of subscription updates to animal magazines and journals, and a few more notifying her of pet trade shows in the area.

Then requests from her clients.

Bob St. John wanted Blunders walked on Thursday. He was a new client and Blunders, a three-year-old dachshund, was sorely in need of Lucy's services.

Bob, loving owner that he was, had been won over by Blunder's pleading looks, and now the dog was carrying a little too much weight. The extra pounds for a larger breed might've been easier to handle, but the dachshund's long body made it more easily prone to herniated discs.

The sooner Blunders got the exercise in, and if Bob stuck to the diet the vet had recommended, Lucy was sure that the little dog would be fine in no time.

"Dear Bob …" she intoned out loud, as she began to type a response confirming the date and time, and set an alert reminder for herself on her phone.

Martha Bigsby wanted Charlie walked every day that week. Charlie was a six-year-old Airedale Terrier. His coat was perfect and thankfully so was his health. He was Martha's prize-winning pooch and she loved him dearly.

Lucy loved owners who shared her appreciation for their animals. Charlie had a big show coming up before the holidays, and she wanted to be sure he was ready for it.

Dear Martha. I confirm that I'll pick up Charlie at seven each morning this week. We can return to our normal nine o'clock slot once you're back from Bakersfield.

She spent the next twenty minutes replying to her work emails before checking her personal ones, though was finished with those in less than one.

Lucy's life consisted mostly of work, and very little of the social aspects that most other people found entertaining. Socialising just wasn't her thing really.

She'd always been happier around animals than people. They, especially dogs, were easy to understand and predictable for the most part.

People weren't, and that was a difficulty for Lucy. She liked what she could rely on and she'd been disappointed far too many times by people.

Never by her furry friends.

Her phone rang then and she checked the caller display. It was Eustacia, her neighbor on the floor below; a woman who believed it was her job to marry off every singleton in their building.

"Lucy? Are you there? Of course, you're there. You're screening my calls aren't you?" Eustacia's Brooklyn accent pierced her ears.

Her new neighbor, who had moved from New York four months ago, was convinced she knew what was best for Lucy, and that she'd find her the 'perfect guy'.

"Trust me. I know all about these things. At home, they used to call me the matchmaker. I can set up anyone with anyone. You leave it to me. A young girl like you shouldn't be all alone every night. It's ain't natural."

Lucy would've appreciated the help, if it weren't for the fact that Eustacia had terrible taste in men.

"Mrs. Abernathy in 4C told me that her son Martin is back in town. And I told her you'd love to meet him. Would you give her a call? She says he'd loved to meet you too."

A perfect example of Eustacia's poor taste: Martin Abernathy was four years older than Lucy. He had a habit of snorting all the time and when she was little, he used to stick gum in her hair.

She rolled her eyes as her neighbor's shrill voice continued. She washed the dishes and put them away, and Eustacia was *still* talking.

Then, finally making her excuses, Lucy hung up the phone and got ready for work.

Her clothing and shoes were comfortable, cosy and most importantly, breathable. There was a *lot* of walking around in her line of work, and no matter what the deodorant companies claimed, she'd rather be safe than sorry.

Dogs were after all, very sensitive to smell.

CHAPTER 2

First, Lucy headed to Olympus Avenue, where one of her charges resided.

While the service was called 12 Dogs, in truth she rarely had as many pooches all at once, but could certainly handle that much.

She also didn't do favorites, and would never admit to having one. Much like people, breeds were individual, and to say you liked dog one better than the other was somewhat unfair. People couldn't help who they were and neither could animals.

However, if Lucy *truly* had to choose a favorite dog – and was absolutely pressed on the matter – she'd pick Berry Cole.

Berry was a five-year-old chocolate brown Labrador and Great Dane mix – a Labradane.

Lucy just called him a sweetie.

He was loyal and loving, and despite his humongous size, being closer in build to his Great Dane mother than his Lab father, he was very gentle.

He was also the perfect choice for his owner, Mrs Cole.

Though Lucy sometimes wondered how the seventy-five-year-old woman managed to feed the colossus.

He was *always* hungry, so much so that Lucy had started carrying extra snacks soon after he'd joined her troop.

Though if she could pick a dog for herself, it couldn't be one as huge as Berry. But that was a moot point, because unfortunately, Lucy's landlord didn't allow pets in the building.

Mrs. Cole was a widow with no children, and Lucy sometimes wondered if that would be her own fate - a life alone.Though at least Mrs. Cole had a canine companion. She didn't even have that.

Now she knocked on the door.

"Morning," Mrs. Cole greeted Lucy with a smile the moment she opened the door. She looked tired today, more so than on most mornings when she called to pick up Berry.

Maybe she was feeling down.

Lucy could bring her back something from Toasties to perk up her spirits. It was the best cafe and pastry store in all of Whitedale, and Mrs. Cole had a thing for their Peppermint Chocolate Croissants.

"Hi, Mrs. Cole. Is he ready?" The words came out in a plume of white. Winter was well and truly here and Christmas now only a couple of weeks away.

They'd had their first heavy snowfall just a few days before and soon, the entirety of Whitedale would be covered in it.

The words had only just left Lucy's mouth, when the big dog came bounding to the door. He rushed past his owner and promptly jumped up and landed his big paws on her chest, knocking her back a step.

"Berry, calm down," Mrs. Cole scolded lightly.

"It's okay," Lucy laughed as Berry licked her face. "He's just happy to see me."

The older woman chuckled. "He always is. I can't contend with him like I used to with this hip. I'm so happy he still gets to go out and have fun when you're around."

"It's my pleasure, and you know I really love this big guy," Lucy chuckled as she removed his paws from her chest and stooped down to scratch behind his ears.

Mrs. Cole duly handed her the leash from by the door and Lucy clipped it in place. She carried spare leashes and clean-up items in her backpack, but it was important to get Berry on the right track from the get-go.

"He's staying out for the whole day, yes?" she confirmed.

"Yes, if that's good with you."

Mrs. Cole was one of the few people Lucy could chat easily to. She supposed it was because she reminded her so much of the grandmother who had raised her.

She didn't have anyone now though. A fact she was well used to, but whenever Christmas came around, it was just that little bit harder to bear.

"Of course. You have a great day," Lucy told Mrs Cole as she began to lead Berry from the porch. "And get back inside, it's cold out. We'll see you later."

"You too," the older woman called after her, chuckling as Lucy struggled to keep pace with the dog. "And don't let the big guy wear you out too much."

CHAPTER 3

The feeling of Christmas was well and truly in the air.

All the stores in town were now fully decorated for the holiday season. Garlands and wreaths were everywhere, twinkling lights in every shop window, and the local tree farm business was booming with a fine selection of firs, pines and spruces.

Lucy wasn't getting a tree though. She never did. It felt wasted when it was just her.

She stopped for a moment to look into the window of Daphne's Dreamland Toy store, smiling automatically at the holiday display. The place was every child's wonderland and had been in existence for over forty years.

Lucy could remember when her mother used to bring her there as a child. The owner, Daphne would give her candy canes whenever she came in.

She was gone now though, just like Lucy's mother.

A deep sadness filled her heart at the memory. Her mom had been a lone parent and her dad was in the military.

They married before being deployed but he never came back. He sent her mother annulment papers a few months later. He'd met someone else where he was stationed and decided that she was the better choice.

Her mother had never quite gotten over it.

A sudden jerk snapped Lucy back to the present as Berry resumed his march toward home.

It was now a little after four in the afternoon, when she usually dropped the dogs back.

Berry was her final drop-off today, and he seemed to know it was past time, because he was trotting toward Olympus so purposefully that she knew only the prospect of food could be drawing him.

"Hey, slow down there, buddy," she commanded gently. "We'll be there soon."

She'd never seen him so determined. It was strange.

"Wait. I'm coming, I'm coming," Lucy called as he rushed to the corner and made a beeline for the street. He jerked hard and she almost tripped on the curb as the leash slipped from her hand, and the big dog ran off.

He disappeared down the street and she rushed after him.

"Hey there big guy …" Lucy heard a voice call out from nearby, and rushing round to Mrs Cole's, she stopped short.

A man, over six feet tall and dressed in jeans, a red plaid shirt, brown jacket and a hardhat, was standing outside the house.

Lucy had never seen him before, but clearly, Berry had.

The dog's paws were planted solidly on the man's chest and he was licking his face eagerly, as his tail wagged behind him. The guy, whoever he was, was laughing heartily at the affection.

Lucy watched the friendly moment like an intruder.

"Hey buddy, where's your mama today, huh? Where is she?" he was asking in a sing-song tone.

It was several seconds before he noticed her and turned to meet her gaze, but when he did Lucy's breath hitched.

He was so handsome. Square jaw with a dimple in his chin. A five o'clock shadow, tanned skin and the most brilliant blue eyes she'd ever seen. He wasn't any Martin Abernathy that was for sure. She could see dark brown hair peeking out from beneath the hardhat.

"Hello," he greeted with a smile, then nodded toward the house. "You looking for Mrs. Cole, too?"

Lucy couldn't speak for several seconds. She just stared at him. This was what always happened when handsome men spoke to her; she completely lost all sense. Her shyness took over and suddenly she became an incoherent nincompoop, her mind completely muddled.

Finally, she found her tongue before she embarrassed herself any further.

"Yes, returning Berry. I'm his dog walker."

He looked at her blankly for a second, and then smiled. "Oh. Are you Lucy?"

She was shocked that he knew her name.

"Yes ..." she stammered. "Who are you?"

He took several steps to close the gap between them and extended his hand with a dazzling smile.

"I'm Scott. Mrs. Cole's contractor. I just finished working on her roof."

Lucy took his hand. "I didn't know she had one," she replied.

"A roof?"

A second of anxiety struck her. "No ... a contractor."

He chuckled. "I was just kidding."

Well done Lucy. Next time, try something simple like 'nice to meet you'.

"Nice to meet you," she mumbled.

"Nice to finally meet you too," he replied as he drew his hand back. He looked at the house and then back to her. "Was she expecting you back now?"

Finally? What did that mean? Did he know her from somewhere? She was certain he couldn't. She'd certainly never seen him before.

Maybe Mrs. Cole had mentioned her. But why?

"Yes. I always bring Berry back around this time. When he stays out all day," she added quickly, when she realized that she hadn't answered.

Berry himself was already at the door scratching to be let in. As always the big guy was ravenous.

"Strange," Scott stated as he turned back to her. "I've been here for a while now, and she hasn't answered. I usually check in on her when I can. I don't like that she's all alone in winter, especially given the darker nights and cold weather. So I try to stop by now and again, just to make sure she's okay."

How sweet.

"She's probably just late getting back from the store or something," he shrugged.

But that didn't make sense to Lucy. Mrs. Cole always made sure she was home when they got there.

She knew how Berry got by that hour of the day. His mind was solely on his dinner and if he didn't get it he got grumpy.

Something wasn't right.

"I have to go," Scott said then. "I've got a meeting with a client over on Hilliard. Could you tell her I stopped by and I'll pass back soon?"

Lucy nodded. "Sure." She turned and watched him walk back to his truck.

Berry attempted to follow him but Lucy grabbed a hold of his leash as he tried to gallop off. "Oh no, you don't Buster. Not this time."

Scott got into the truck and then turned back to wave in their direction as he drove off. "See you around, Lucy."

She waved back, still slightly dazed by the unexpected encounter. "See you around."

CHAPTER 4

But the minute Scott was out of sight, Lucy's thoughts loosened, and a niggling discomfort began to fill her stomach.

She turned back to the quiet house. There was no sound of Christmas music coming from inside. Mrs. Cole loved this time of year and she always left festive music playing - even when she went out.

"Nope. Something's not right."

Lucy walked toward the door and took the steps two at a time. She rang the doorbell.

Nothing. She knocked. Still nothing.

"Mrs. Cole?" she called out. No answer.

She looked at Berry. He was scratching at the door and whining a little.

"Let's try the back ..." Lucy mused, as she led him from the porch and around the side of the house to check the rear kitchen window.

Inside, everything was dark and quiet.

"This isn't at all like her ...." she muttered to herself. She knocked on the back door too.

Still nothing.

"Maybe Mrs. Stillman knows where she might be?" she mumbled to Berry, as she headed back out front and next door to the neighbor's house.

Mrs. Stillman was a cat lover. The sound of mewing greeted Lucy the second she stepped onto her property. She looked up at the box window and saw a marmalade tabby looking back at her as she approached the door and knocked.

The owner answered a few seconds later. Her face looked drawn and her grey and her red hair was slightly disheveled. She looked down at Berry and her face fell.

"Hi Mrs. Stillman. I was just over at Mrs. Cole's to drop Berry back, but she doesn't seem to be home yet, which is unusual. Would you by any chance know where she is?"

The other woman's expression became more solemn by the second, and a further sense of foreboding began to slither into Lucy's heart.

The neighbor sighed. "I don't know how to tell you this Lucy, but Sonia passed away earlier today. I only just got back from the hospital."

Lucy's hearing had become hollow. The words being spoken weren't real. They didn't make sense.

Mrs. Cole couldn't be ... *dead*.

She had only left her a few hours ago, smiling and fine. Yes, the older woman had mentioned she felt tired, but she seemed in good health.

How could she be dead?

"How ...?"

"We're not sure. They suspect that it may have been an aneurysm in her sleep," Mrs. Stillman explained. "I went over earlier to drop off a pecan pie I'd made. She really loved my pecan pie," she added through tears.

Tears were filling Lucy's eyes too. She looked at Berry. His mama was gone, but of course he had no idea.

What was going to become of him?

"When I didn't hear her answer I knew something was wrong," Mrs. Stillman continued. "I called the ambulance right off. When we went in, she was in her bed in that nice floral dress she got a few weeks ago."

Lucy could only nod. If she tried to speak she'd start sobbing and she couldn't let herself do that.

It had been so long since she'd lost someone she cared about, and Mrs. Cole's death hurt almost as much as her grandmother's had.

"Thank you for telling me, Mrs. Stillman." She forced the words from her lips. "I'll be going now."

The other woman nodded her understanding as Lucy turned to leave.

She couldn't believe this was happening. She walked back to the house and took a seat on the porch steps.

Berry sat beside her and promptly lay his big head in her lap. He looked up at her pleadingly.

"I know you're hungry Big Guy, but I can't get you food just yet," she told him. She stroked the top of his head gently. "You're mama's gone, buddy. Mrs. Cole won't be able to take care of you anymore."

Berry let out a whine, as if he understood.

Lucy knew that science would say that he was just picking up on her emotions, but she guessed deep down that animals understood a great deal more than people gave them credit for.

CHAPTER 5

❄

Lucy waited for over an hour for someone to come to the house, feeding Berry the remainder of the food she kept in her backpack.

The family of people who died usually came by to check on things, didn't they?

It was then she remembered that Mrs. Cole's niece, Joy, had moved to California a few months ago.

She had no family in town anymore. No one was coming.

What was she going to do with Berry?

Lucy walked back to Mrs. Stillman's.

"Me again," she said as the other woman answered the door.

"Lucy, what are you still doing here?"

"I was waiting for someone from Mrs. Cole's family to come, so I can give them Berry, but then I remembered that Joy moved."

"Months ago."

"Right, that's the problem. There's nowhere for me to take him," she explained nervously.

"I see. What are you going to do?"

Lucy forced a smile as she gave Mrs. Stillman a pleading look. "I was kind of hoping that maybe he could stay here for a bit..."

"No."

"Just for the night, even?"

"I'm sorry, but - "

"Please, Mrs. Stillman. He has nowhere to go. I'd take him home with me in a heartbeat, but animals aren't allowed in my building. He just needs someplace to spend the night. I promise tomorrow I'll find a more suitable situation. I promise." She raised three fingers in the air. "Brownie promise."

It was the best she could offer.

The other woman looked at her and then at Berry and then at the cat that was curling round her ankles.

"Fine, but just for the night. He can stay out back and I'll get some food from next door."

Lucy gave a huge internal sigh of relief. "Thank you."

"Just overnight," the woman insisted. "I don't like dogs, Lucy. They're too much trouble. Cats, they're independent. A lot easier to handle."

Lucy nodded. She didn't care what Mrs. Stillman preferred as long as Berry had someplace to sleep tonight.

"I'll be back tomorrow morning, I swear."

"What time?"

"Is seven good for you?" she asked handing over Berry's leash, and giving him a reassuring rub around the ears.

"Seven sharp."

"I'll be there."

CHAPTER 6

Next, Lucy went to work on her landlord.

"Please Mr. Wells. Mrs. Cole is gone and Berry has no one to take care of him."

"What's that got to do with me?"

He was short and Lucy was sure, jealous of everything that could possibly be as tall as him. Which was why animals were a problem too. Their character was greater than his height.

"If you could bend the rule on pets in the building just this once, I could bring Berry here and take care of him until I can make arrangements with Mrs. Cole's family."

"Absolutely not. If I bend it for you I have to bend it for everyone, and then my entire building is overrun with furballs and fleas. No thank you."

"It won't be like that," she assured him.

"My answer is still no."

"Won't you reconsider - please? It's Christmas," Lucy asked, but the look on his face made her stop.

He wasn't changing his mind for her or anyone, no matter what time of the year it was.

She'd just have to find another way.

Berry was too large for her apartment anyway. He deserved a big house and garden, like Mrs. Cole's, where he could run around and have space.

She went to pick up Berry at seven just as she promised.

Mrs. Stillman looked frazzled.

She informed Lucy that Berry had whined all night and she'd hardly slept a wink.

Even worse, it had upset all of her six cats and they'd done a number on her couch in response.

Lucy couldn't apologize enough as she took the leash from her and led Berry away. The further away they both were, the better.

She'd figure something out.

She then took Berry and her other charges for their usual walk to McGivney Park.

It was one of the few places they could be off their leashes, and all the dogs loved it there.

Once they arrived, Lucy unhooked their collars and let them run around and have fun while she sat on a nearby bench watching.

The only one who wasn't allowed off leash was Pegasus. The black and white Japanese Chin had a habit of running away.

She didn't like playing with the other dogs and Lucy was convinced that it was because Pegasus thought herself better than running around in a park.

She looked at the other dogs with such an air of condescension it was always better to keep her close.

She and Perdita, Mr. Cross's Dalmatian, were always

yapping at each other. Perdita didn't like Pegasus one bit and more often than not, Lucy had to act the go-between.

Now, she put her phone to her ear again as she tried to sort out her most pressing problem.

"Hello? Is this Joy?" Lucy had called every Joy Reese she could find in the directory, until she finally reached the right one.

"Yes."

"You don't know me, but I'm Lucy Adams. I take care of Berry the dog, for your aunt, Mrs. Cole." She nodded solemnly as Joy explained that her aunt had passed away. "Yes, I know. That's why I called. You see, Berry is going to need someplace to live and I was hoping that you could take him."

"I can't," the woman replied quickly.

Lucy's heart sank. "May I ask why not?"

"Look, my aunt loved that dog but I don't. I don't do pets and I have no intention of taking on such a responsibility. And that dog is HUGE."

"I know he's on the bigger side, but truly, Berry is such a sweetie that you'd have no trouble at all."

"I don't think you understand. I don't want to try. I just don't want a dog. It doesn't work for me, or my lifestyle."

Lucy's heart was plummeting rapidly every second that went by. "So what should I do with him?"

"I don't know to be honest. Sorry, but I have my aunt's funeral to prepare for at the moment. I can't deal with what's going to happen to some dog. I'm sorry, but I can't help you."

With that, the line disconnected and Lucy stared blankly at her phone, shocked. She couldn't believe the stance Joy had taken to the idea of caring for Berry.

He was such a wonderful dog. How could she feel that way about him - how could anyone?

Lucy knew that the woman's feelings were shared by many others in the world, but she'd never personally experienced anyone express such outright dislike before.

She was quite stunned, frankly. But still the problem remained. What was she going to do now?

There was no choice.

Clearly it was up to Lucy to find Berry a new home, and soon.

CHAPTER 7

Later, she took the other dogs back to their owners, and then took Berry along to Toasties.

They had free wifi and Lucy used that and Betsy her PC to make up some fliers. It took her several tries to get the wording just the way she wanted, but in the end, she was pleased with her efforts.

"What do you think?" she asked as she turned the screen for Berry to see. He raised his nose and sniffed the laptop before losing interest. "What? You don't like it?"

Lucy finished her snack and then emailed the flier to the print shop, ordering up a batch of thirty.

She'd pick them up and plaster them around town.

Hopefully, some prospects would give her a call and Berry would have a new home sooner rather than later.

The print shop had her copies ready by the time she arrived. She'd used festive graphics and snapped a cute picture of Berry, wanting the flier to stand out.

No one was going to miss it.

Lucy began to staple fliers on every pole and post in town

she could find. She asked a few store owners if she could post some in their windows and they allowed her to do so.

"Hey, what's that?" a boy asked as she stapled her last to a lamp post.

"It's a flier."

"For what?" He had to be about five. A curious age.

Lucy stooped down to his height.

"It's to try and find a home for this dog," she explained as Berry moved closer.

He stretched his head forward to sniff the boy but the little kid recoiled.

"Don't worry. He won't hurt you," Lucy assured him.

"He's so big," he gasped in wonder. "He must cost a lot of money."

"Actually, I'm not selling him; I'm giving him away to whoever can give him a good home," she explained.

"Why?" the boy asked. "Don't you like him?"

She chuckled. "I like him a lot, but he's not mine. The lady who owned him sadly died so now he needs a home. I have to find a new owner for him in time for Christmas."

"That's sad. My dog Ruffles died too. What's his name?"

"He's Berry," Lucy continued as she patted his side gently. "He's a Labradane."

"A what?"

She started to laugh just as a tall blonde woman called out. "Tobey?"

"Is that your mom?" Lucy asked gently. The smile was still teasing her lips.

He nodded.

"I think she's calling you. You should probably go to her."

The boy smiled. He was missing a front tooth. He took off running.

"Mommy! Mommy! That lady over there is giving away a dog for Christmas. Can I have him?"

But by the outright horrified look on his mom's face at the dog's size, Lucy was certain little Tobey, and unfortunately Berry too, was on to a loser.

THE FLIERS DISAPPEARED FASTER than expected and soon, Lucy was exhausted.

"Let's see how it goes overnight," she told Berry as he trotted skittishly beside her. "You never know who might see them. If we don't have any luck, then I'll order up a few more and head further outside of town."

Berry barked happily and Lucy wished it was because he agreed, but she knew it was probably only because he wanted the snack in her pocket.

She took one out and tossed it to him when her phone rang.

Lucy didn't recognize the number. "Hello? Yes, this *is* who you call about the dog," she repeated cheerfully, giving Berry an excited smile. "Yes, of course, you can. Are you free now?"

The call was short, but to the point. The Emersons from Crichton Corner were looking for a dog and saw her flier in one of the shop windows just now. They were interested in Berry.

Excitement filled her chest as she began to walk in the direction of Taylor's Arts and Things.

The family had been buying supplies for their daughter's school project when they saw the flier. They were a young couple with a child, which was perfect. Labradanes were family dogs and great with children.

Lucy was very hopeful that the Emersons might be the answer to her prayers.

She saw them immediately as she approached.

Mrs. Emerson was a few inches shorter than her husband. They were both blondes, fair skinned and wrapped up snuggly in matching plaid scarves.

"Mr. and Mrs. Emerson," she greeted with a smile as she got closer.

"Lucy?"

"Yes. And this is Berry," she said as she and Berry got closer.

Mrs. Emerson's eyes grew to twice the size.

"This is … it?" She looked at her husband.

Lucy frowned. "Is something wrong?"

"Not really, it's just … we thought he would be smaller," she said. Her speech was stilted and Lucy was confused.

"Haven't you ever seen a Labradane before?"

"No, we just saw the picture on the flier and thought he looked sweet," she explained. "I'm sorry. We live in a small house with no backyard. We don't have the space."

"We're really sorry to have bothered you," her husband added, smiling pitifully. "Thanks for coming."

Lucy's hopes were falling off a cliff, and that was all he had to say?

It wasn't his fault though, she thought disheartened.

Maybe she should've put something in the picture to give people an idea of his size.

Sadly, Lucy couldn't think of anything that could convey the dog's big heart too.

CHAPTER 8

Two more days passed and still Lucy had no luck in her quest, other than getting a break from Mrs. Stillman who'd agreed to let the big dog stay with her a little longer, but only at night.

It wasn't long before more people noticed the fliers though.

The town was small and some already knew Berry as being Mrs. Cole's dog, and were keen to take him in given his sweet temperament, but once Lucy met with such prospects she realized that the trouble wasn't him, so much as it was them.

Most didn't have the space for a dog his size. Others weren't up to his care, or they couldn't afford the cost associated with such a large (and hungry) breed.

She was surprised that there was even one who had an issue with Lucy not being able to provide papers to ensure the purity of Berry's parents.

Others were like Mrs. Cole, older and infirm. Not ideal.

She'd endured repeated hopes and repeated let-downs,

and was beyond frustrated by the time she finished talking to the Ruprechts.

They were really nice people, but were planning a move in a few months, and given they were relocating to Denver city, it didn't make sense.

They'd merely find themselves in the same position Lucy was now. Such a temporary arrangement wasn't fair to Berry.

Now, Lucy was dreading having to go back to Mrs. Stillman to ask for even more time, but she had no choice.

Mrs. Cole's neighbor was waiting for her when she arrived. The look on her face was laced with disapproval.

"I take it that you still haven't found a place?"

Lucy shook her head despondently. "No. I tried. They were good people, but just not the right fit."

"I can tell you what's not the right fit – that dog in my house. I've lost two lamps already. I'll have to remove the carpet in the back room where he sleeps, and honestly my cats are so unnerved that it's driving me nuts. I can't keep him anymore, Lucy. I'm sorry. I really am, but I can't do it anymore. Christmas is on the way and my house is a disaster zone. I can't clean it because of that … *beast*, and my family's going to be arriving for the holidays soon. He has to go."

"Please Mrs. Stillman, just give me a few more days. Like you say, Christmas is the on the way and Berry needs a home in time for then - the right home. I still have a few more leads," she pleaded.

"This is it, Lucy. Absolute last time. You get three days, and then he's out of here, or I take him to the shelter myself. I mean it." She took the leash from Lucy who watched as a sorrowful-looking Berry disappeared inside.

Clearly he was enjoying his stay here just as much as Mrs. Stillman.

Three days?

Lucy couldn't - *wouldn't* - consider the local shelter. It just wasn't and had never been an option. She loved the big guy too much and could never abandon him that way.

But what was she supposed to do?

Lucy was fast-becoming all out of options.

CHAPTER 9

Sunset Trail was the most picturesque spot in Whitedale and perfect for dog-walking.

It was why Lucy liked going there so much. Lots of quiet space and room to roam between the trees, along the meandering landscape and with a view of Treasure Lake that was unsurpassed.

Sunlight reflected on beautiful blue water like diamonds and gold, which was how it got its name.

Set on a gentle winding slope, the trail was a criss-cross of paths along Lonesome Ridge, Whitedale's diminutive mountain.

Every day she took the dogs there, weather permitting; the park being for days when the forecast wasn't so great or the likelihood of rain was imminent.

Though right now Lucy felt as if she was walking under a cloud, but at least the weather was clear.

There was absolutely no one left on her prospects list.

Mrs. Stillman was adamant that Berry was going to have to leave soon and there was no place else for Lucy to put him.

She'd gone back to her landlord again, begging him, but that was a waste of time. The local vet couldn't help either; none of his regulars were looking for a new dog and he wasn't prepared to even temporarily house an animal of Berry's size.

She was well and truly stuck.

Oscar, Mr. Reese's Alsatian was trotting beside her. Perdita was jumping all over her new boyfriend Pongo. Mrs. Cross figured her precious lady was lonely and thought it a good idea to get her someone to play with. She needed to hold back a little on the whole *101 Dalmatians* thing.

Lucy's mind was so cluttered. She wanted to keep Berry in town, someplace he knew, someplace where the landscape was familiar.

There had to be *something* she could do to help.

Her thoughts were so scattered that she didn't realize she'd wandered off their usual path. It was only when snowflakes began to fall that she glanced up to see that it was darker than it should be.

The trees seemed much closer now, and the overhanging foliage thicker; blocking out the light.

It was then Lucy realized that she was on unfamiliar terrain. With all her musing, she'd allowed the dogs to lead her deeper into the woods.

A sense of panic began to rise up in her stomach now, as cold wind sliced through the trees, making her shiver a little.

"Where are we guys?" she mumbled.

Lucy looked in every direction, but nothing seemed familiar, and she couldn't tell which way the lake was, finding it even harder to get her bearings.

The dogs hovered around her. They wanted to keep going but she didn't know which direction they should turn.

Maybe if we just go back the way we came?

She turned to do so, but at this point couldn't figure out which direction they'd come here from.

This was ... not good.

"Keep calm Lucy. Nothing to worry about. You just need to keep walking. You'll find something," she told herself.

Trying to use her cellphone was pointless; there was no signal on this trail - another reason it was so perfect. You could escape the outside world while you were there, and just enjoy the scenery and the quiet solitude.

But of course that wasn't much help to her now.

She was at a loss, when Berry suddenly turned to the right and barked.

Lucy's gaze snapped in the direction he was looking.

"What? Is there something over there?"

The big dog barked again and began to pull away from her, his tail wagging rapidly now.

Well, if there was something over there that had him reacting in that way, then like it or not, they were going in that direction.

Lead the way, Big Dog.

CHAPTER 10

The snow began to fall harder as Lucy and the other dogs hurried along with Berry leading the way.

The older ones were amusing themselves by jumping on one another and sniffing the unfamiliar territory.

All Lucy wanted was to see something she recognized. Once she did she'd feel as happy and carefree as they were.

She checked her watch. If she didn't find a way back soon, the owners would be unhappy. She was always right on time dropping back their pets. Timekeeping was important to her, and them.

If she was very late dropping them back today, how was she going to explain it? What effect would it have on her business?

When Lucy was scared of one thing suddenly there seemed to be a million more things to worry about as well.

She was still following Berry when something glinted in the distance.

Lucy squinted and tried to make out what it was. It took her a minute to realize it was the sun reflecting on a window.

Relief swept over her. If there was a window, then there was a house. If there was a house, then maybe there was someone home.

Someone who could point them in the right direction.

The second the house came into view, Berry began to bark more. He ran toward it as if it were calling him.

Lucy couldn't hold on to him and all the others too.

The dogs' combined strength was a lot to deal with, especially when Berry was so eager. He'd excited the pack, and the task of calming them all wasn't something she needed right now.

Besides, she could see where he was going, so she figured she might as well just let him lead the way.

Releasing him off the leash, Lucy hurried the other animals along behind Berry. The snow was really coming down now. At least the house would be a good place to shelter for a bit, if nothing else.

They broke through the trees into a clearing around the property. The first thing that struck Lucy was the state of the building. It looked abandoned, though the house itself wasn't dilapidated.

Why would anyone leave a nice place in such a gorgeous location unattended?

The site had an uninterrupted view of the lake, and there wasn't another home to be found as far as the eye could see.

It was double-height, lodge-cabin style; a combination of stone and wood. A gabled roof and huge window panes maximized the natural light and the beautiful surroundings.

The land around it was cleared, as if the owner intended to put in a lawn or maybe a flowerbed, but there was nothing there now.

To one side was a deck that extended out into a jetty on

the water.

It was Lucy's dream house.

She walked closer and quickly realized that the place wasn't abandoned, like she'd first thought. It was in fact, under construction. The roof on the far side of the porch was half completed.

And perfect for sheltering beneath out of the snow, at least for now.

"Come on guys," Lucy urged as she began to jog to the house.

The dogs followed happily as they tried to keep up.

By now she was cold and her breath was coming out as white mist with every exhalation.

"Berry!" she called as she got closer. "Wait, hold on!"

Of course, the big guy didn't wait, and instead raced around the side of the house.

Lucy safely secured the other dogs to a nearby post before going in search of him.

There was construction material lying around everywhere, stuff that she didn't have the first clue about, but her primary focus was finding Berry.

"Berry, come here boy," she called out again.

Then a sound from somewhere nearby caught her attention and she walked around the porch to find Berry standing over someone lying on the ground; the dog's face buried in their neck, and his tail wagging a mile-a-minute.

"Berry!"

For a moment she was horrified, but then realized that the person's hands weren't fending the dog off, but rubbing his coat and scratching his fur.

And when that person turned in the direction of her voice, Lucy realized to her surprise that she recognized who it was.

CHAPTER 11

"Scott?'

The same dazzling eyes that had so befuddled her that first day they met, now turned in Lucy's direction, having the same effect on her as they did the first time.

Berry noticed her then too, and the big pooch came bounding back to her.

She laid a calming hand on his back as he panted by her side.

Scott pushed up from the ground, covered in what looked like sawdust and with a big smile on his face.

"Lucy, what are you doing here?" he asked as he dusted himself off.

"I could ask you the same thing," she replied reattaching Berry's leash and keeping a firm grip on it.

Scott's presence explained at least why the big dog had been so drawn to the house. He'd obviously picked up the scent of his friend from the trees.

Thank goodness.

"I live here," he answered and chuckled when Lucy glanced

skeptically at the house. "I know, it's a mess. Who could live here, right? I mean, it's my place, but I haven't moved in permanently - not yet. The house is still under construction as you can probably tell. I've been working on it for about a year now."

"By yourself?" Lucy couldn't betray her surprise. The thought that he'd done all this on his own was impressive.

"Yes. I started the construction as a pet project and I'd hoped to have it done a long time ago, but business picked up and I had so much work backing up for other people that it sort of got put on ice." He looked at the house and gave a rueful smile.

"It's a really beautiful place. Anyone would love to live here."

"You think so?"

"Definitely. I would for sure," she added with a nervous chuckle, then coughed when she realized how weird that may have sounded.

Thankfully the sound of the other pooches' impatient whining drew their attention.

"Do you have more dogs with you?" Scott asked as he and Lucy moved back toward the porch.

"Yes. I'm really sorry to intrude. I was walking them in the woods and we got lost. Berry is the one who led us here. I tied the others to the porch so I could go look for him," she explained.

The snowfall was thickening quickly as they stepped back on to the porch and the dogs were circling around agitatedly. They could feel the bad weather coming, Lucy suspected.

She needed to get them home.

"Could you tell me the fastest way to get back to town from here?" she asked Scott, as he headed toward the others and stooped to greet them, patting their heads and rubbing their coats.

They were all friendly dogs who welcomed strangers and seemed *very* pleased with Scott's attention.

And by the delighted look on his face, clearly the feeling was mutual.

He glanced up at the sky. "There's no going back to town until the weather clears, and certainly not on foot," he stated. "This isn't going to let up anytime soon."

Lucy looked pained. "So we're stuck?"

"Looks like it," he replied. "Weather changes quickly up on the trail. Usually doesn't last long, but a cold snap can lead to some serious snowfall, and it is that time of year. You guys are welcome to stay here until it passes, though."

"Oh no, we couldn't impose …" Lucy protested.

"Don't be silly, it's no imposition. If anything you'd be doing me a favor."

"How so?"

"If you stay and shelter here, you make me feel better knowing that guys are safe. Plus, if you do, I can give you a ride back when the worst clears."

The proposition was tempting, and the thought of making their way back to town in this snow wasn't one Lucy relished.

Chances were there was cellphone reception at Scott's house too, so she could keep the owners informed of their pets' whereabouts.

Plus Lucy kind of wanted to see what the inside of the house looked like.

"Okay," she conceded, smiling gratefully. "Thank you."

CHAPTER 12

❄

Scott welcomed them all inside the house, leading Lucy to an enclosed rear room that was unfinished, but insulated from the outside.

She settled the dogs there before following him in to the kitchen which was partially furnished, but seemed fully operational.

"Hot chocolate?" he asked as he approached the stove. He turned on a burner and placed a small pot over the flame.

"Yes, please. I love hot chocolate."

She watched as Scott poured heavy cream into the pot and dropped several chunks of chocolate into it. He added several other things too but she couldn't tell what they were.

"Please don't go to any trouble - I actually thought you meant the powdered kind," she insisted, watching him work.

"Not in this house. My mom was the kind of woman who liked to make things from scratch," he smiled as he stirred the contents. "She taught me well. Marshmallows?"

Lucy couldn't help but smile. "Is it even hot chocolate if there isn't?"

When the chocolate was ready, Scott poured it into two large mugs and set one on the table in front of her, adding several huge marshmallows on top. "Enjoy."

She sipped the warm, creamy liquid and hummed her approval. "It's delicious."

"Thanks. Mom's recipe."

"So is she going to live with you here too?" she queried conversationally.

"No. She died a few years ago."

"I'm so sorry."

"It's OK," he assured her easily. "How about you? Does your family live in town?"

"No," Lucy confessed. "It's just me. I don't have any family."

"I know how that is." He raised his mug to her and winked. "I guess here's to us loners then."

"Cheers."

"How is Mrs. Cole?" he asked, as he sipped his chocolate. They were sitting facing each other at the table and Lucy almost spit out her chocolate at the question.

"You mean you haven't heard?" Sadness reared up inside her afresh.

"Heard what?" Scott asked with a hint of alarm.

"Poor Mrs. Cole died last week."

The expression on his face was nothing short of stunned.

"I ... had no idea. I was supposed to come back but I've been working flat out nearly every day coming up to the holidays. I was actually planning to go see her tomorrow. I can't believe it."

"She actually passed the day I met you," Lucy informed him. "An aneurysm, apparently."

"I can't believe it. She was such a sweet old lady and so tough. I kinda thought she'd live forever."

"I know," Lucy felt fresh tears brim at the corner of her eyes.

"So what's going to happen to Berry?" he asked, and she wished he hadn't reminded her of that all too pressing problem.

"I have no idea," she said sighing. "I've been trying so hard to find someone to take him since then, but I've run out of options. He's been with Mrs. Stillman up to now, but she can't handle him anymore. She says I have a couple more days and after that, he's out."

"No one wants to adopt an awesome dog like Berry?" Scott asked, surprised.

"No, that's just it. There were some people interested, but they weren't suitable. They didn't have enough space or they were too old, or simply hadn't thought it through."

"You really care about him."

"Of course I do. He's a great dog, and such a sweetie too, as you know. I love taking care of him. Mrs. Cole loved him, and that's why I need to make sure he goes to someone she'd approve of. I can't just give him to anyone. I need to make sure he'd be happy."

She'd run off on a tangent. It happened sometimes. Now, Scott was just staring at her with a thoughtful look on his face.

"So no one's good enough," he said as he sipped his chocolate again.

Lucy blushed. "I guess so. It's just, I'd hate for him to go to someone who wouldn't love him as Mrs. Cole did. Someone who wouldn't treat him right. I haven't been successful yet, but I'm sure I'm going to find someone, the perfect someone for him."

"I understand. I have a few rescues myself I'm hoping to

rehome with the right people, but I haven't had a chance to start looking yet."

Lucy looked up, interested. "Rescue dogs?"

"Yes, four little guys I came across while on the job. Lou Lou, I found down on Weston. She's an American English Coonhound I saw wandering the woods a few weeks ago. She didn't have a collar or any way to identify her, so I think she may have belonged to some hunters who left her behind. Some people just don't care for their pets the way they should."

"I know. I can't stand it. I just don't understand how you can treat any living thing with such disrespect." Lucy smiled then. "That breeds's a really sweet animal too. Very amiable."

"I know," Scott grinned. "Whenever she sees me, it's like coming home to a friend."

"She's here?" Lucy asked, surprised. She hadn't seen any animals when she came in and wondered where they were.

"I have a kennel out back. I built it because I hope to one day get some Leonbergers, or maybe a Neapolitan Mastiff."

Lucy's heart was backflipping in her chest. Neapolitan Mastiffs? They were such huge, beautiful animals. She'd always wanted to see one up-close but had never had the chance. They were also very expensive dogs and required a lot of care.

"Well, whenever you do get them I'd love to be your walker," she offered genuinely.

"I'll keep that in mind."

"So, you were telling me about Lou Lou?" Lucy got back to the topic at hand. "You know, in terms of rehoming her, a dog like that needs someone who can help stimulate its hunting nature. It wouldn't be fair to have her cooped up in a house. You wouldn't want a novice having her either. Breaking her in, if she's not already broken, will be a lot of trouble for someone who doesn't know what they're doing. Coonhounds are stubborn and tenacious. They take a little working with, but once they're settled they're just perfect."

He grinned. "You really know a lot about dogs, don't you?"

"Yes," she chuckled bashfully. "I once thought of studying to be a vet when I moved back home from the city, but I gave that idea up pretty quickly. Being a dog walker works best for me right now, but once I get everything in order you'll see. I have big plans for 12 Dogs."

Scott chuckled. "I don't doubt that for a second."

"So what else are you keeping out there?"

"Well there's ET, a male Kelpie."

Lucy tried not to laugh at the names Scott had given his rescues. "A good dog, but they get lonely very quickly. Needs someone who can be with them as much as possible. It's a working dog, bred to be active. Shouldn't be kept inside, and needs to get lots of exercise. I mean *lots*."

Scott kept grinning at her as she espoused the traits of each breed, and who would be the most suitable owner for them.

"You're really good at that you know, matching dogs to the right kind of people."

Lucy shrugged. "I guess. I just know my breeds."

"Have you ever heard of a place called Lisdoonvarna?"

"No. Where is that? Slovakia?"

"Ireland. They have a festival there every summer called the Lisdoonvarna Matchmaking Festival. It's apparently Europe's biggest singles event. Great fun."

"You've been?" Lucy asked, mostly surprised that Scott might be single.

"Yes, earlier this year. Some friends and I were there for a vacation and heard about it. It's been going on for over a hundred and sixty years."

"That's a long time."

"It is. They have this matchmaker guy who, the myth says, if you touch his book with both hands you'll be married within six months." Scott chuckled and drained his mug. "I don't know about that though."

"What? You don't believe that stuff like that can happen?"

"Not really. It's nice to think and to hope for, but I think you and I would have better luck hitting one of the bars." He grinned.

Lucy was intrigued. Then her eyes grew wide. What was he suggesting? Was Scott implying that she needed to go out and get matched?

Suddenly she was embarrassed and uncomfortable again.

"So what does that have to do with me?" she asked hesitantly.

"You could be Whitedale's matchmaker. But instead of people, you could match dogs to potential owners. Turn it into something fun."

There was a novel thought. A dog matchmaking service? It would certainly be a unique addition to her business. And unlike her matchmaking neighbour Eustasia, Lucy understood her customer at least.

Also felt nice that Scott thought she had a talent.

The problem was, Lucy thought ruefully, at the moment she couldn't seem to utilise it for poor Berry.

Or could she?

CHAPTER 13

❄

"So how do you think I should I go about something like this ... for Berry, I mean?" she asked thoughtfully.

She liked what Scott was saying, but the mechanics of it was the question.

"Well," he sat forward in his seat. "I guess you begin like you've just done verbally with me - come up with a kind of ... profile, like a dating profile, listing Berry's canine personality traits, and a corresponding list of preferable qualities in an owner. And maybe my brood too, if you wanted to make a thing of it."

She nodded. "But how do I let people know about it?" She didn't relish the idea of posting up more fliers all around town.

"Well, Christmas is the perfect time to get the whole community interested and involved. You could maybe even open a booth or something."

"12 Dogs of Christmas..." Lucy's brain suddenly kicked into high gear.

"Yes, perfect. I love it! See, you *are* good at this stuff."

Suddenly, she was on a roll. "We can clean Berry and the dogs up, maybe put a bow and some festive ribbons on them and take some photos for their profiles? Set up a doggie matchmaking service to find them their forever homes in time for Christmas. A booth at the Christmas fair would be perfect."

"Yes," Scott was nodding enthusiastically. "All those people in one place all at once. If not from here, then maybe even McKinley? Every year people come over for the tree lighting ceremony. Lots of potential matches. Our own matchmaking festival here in Whitedale, except for dogs."

The grin on Lucy's face wouldn't subside. She *loved* this idea. And, most importantly, it truly could be the perfect opportunity to find Berry *his* perfect match in time for the holidays. Scott's ingenuity had once again set a fire under her and motivated her to keep going.

But what was she going to do with him in the meantime? Lucy remembered then, suddenly crestfallen once more.

The Christmas fair was days away, and she still needed somewhere to keep him.

"Sounds great in theory, but what do I do with Berry until then?" she mused out loud.

Scott shrugged. "Why don't I keep him here?"

"You?"

"Yes, why not? I have plenty of space, plus I already know Berry. And I think he likes me. We get along pretty well, don't you think?"

She smiled. "That you do."

"Can I get you a refil?" he asked, as he got to his feet with his mug in hand.

"No thanks, I'd better get going," Lucy looked at her watch, suddenly realizing the time. Scott was so easy and interesting to talk to the time seemed to have just flown by.

She looked out the window; the snowfall had eased, but the sun was disappearing fast. "I really have to get the dogs home …" She jumped to her feet.

"Right," Scott replied. "That's a shame. I almost forgot you were on the job."

"Me too." She gave him a rueful smile. "It was really nice of you to let us stay this long."

"My pleasure," he answered as he washed the mugs and set them on the drainer. Then he shook the water from his hands and grabbed a towel to dry them. "Let's get you guys home."

BEFORE THEY LEFT, Scott took Berry out back to the kennel he'd told Lucy about, and to introduce her to the other dogs he'd rescued.

It was a big area with plenty of space for them all to run around in, and the kennels themselves were heated and spacious. It was perfect for the big dog and a lifesaver for Lucy. And Mrs Stillman too, no doubt.

She stooped down beside Berry to say goodbye, and he licked her face happily.

"I've got to go now buddy," Lucy said hugging him gently. "Scott's going to take care of you for a little while, but I promise I'll come back to visit you," she said, then looked up at Scott, a little embarrassed for assuming. "If that's OK?"

He smiled. "I wouldn't have it any other way."

CHAPTER 14

❄

The following morning, Lucy woke with sunshine on her face.

Not literally, but it felt that way.

Thanks to Scott's idea and his kind offer to help Berry, she had a spring in her step and a huge weight off her mind.

She bounded out of bed, did her stretches and never had a better tasting bowl of cereal. She finger-combed her hair into a high ponytail, and brushed her teeth while dancing to cheery Christmas songs on the radio.

As expected, Mrs. Stillman was over the moon to learn that Berry would no longer be an occupant in her house. The timing was perfect too because her family had called to inform her that they'd be coming for the holidays a day earlier, leaving her with no choice but to boot him out.

Disaster averted, just in time.

Lucy picked up her usual charges for their walk and the morning seemed to go by quicker, but that might've been because she was so inspired and eager to get cracking with Scott's dog matchmaking idea.

It really was such a brainwave, and sure to be fun, too.

By lunchtime, things were already started to fall into place. She called the town's fair committee and spoke to Mary Winter, the overly enthusiastic community organizer who loved all things Christmas.

Mary was always the first one in town to hang out decorations, and she prided herself on having 'the best' Christmas Cookies on sale at the fair. They were, too.

Lucy was over the moon at her response to the idea of the matchmaking booth. She also happened to be one of the world's biggest dog-lovers, so the idea of helping some down-on-their-luck pups find a home for Christmas was something Mary was deeply enthusiastic about.

"12 Dogs of Christmas is a *great* name for a booth, Lucy. I love it!" she cooed delightedly.

So, she had the permission she needed. But now, Lucy had some groundwork to do.

Berry would be happy at Scott's place for a couple of days, a fantastic temporary solution.

She was determined to have a happy home for him soon, and was also enjoying the prospect of helping Scott out in return.

You really had to love dogs to pick up and take care of strays, not to mention assume the responsibility of rehoming them.

And Lucy really wanted to help him find his rescues their forever homes. He'd already done a lot for these pups by taking them in and caring for them.

It showed real heart.

Once she'd dropped all the dogs back that afternoon, she

picked up her cell and dialed the number Scott had given her the night before, giddily pacing her kitchen as she told him about her progress thus far.

And when he suggested she come by his place to plan things further, visit Berry and take him for his walk, Lucy couldn't deny that she was equally enthused about seeing them both.

CHAPTER 15

❄

It took her a little while to find her way back to Scott's this time, which was around the back of Lonesome Ridge.

Lucy still couldn't believe she'd wandered so far off the path as to find her way to his house in the first place.

Thank goodness for Berry and his sensitive nose.

The house was even more stunning in full daylight against a clear blue sky.

Scott had finished a project earlier that week thus was home again, working on the house.

"Hey there," Lucy called out as she got out of her red Chevy pick-up. He turned and waved at her from the roof, a bright smile lighting up his handsome features.

"I see you found your way back on wheels this time."

"Yep, better prepared," she chuckled as she watched him climb down a ladder.

"You want to see Berry and the others first?" he asked. "Give you a chance to get to know them a little."

"That'd be great."

"So how's your day been?" he asked as they walked side-by-side to the rear of the property.

"Couldn't be better," Lucy replied. "I was out earlier and my thoughts were going a mile a minute. I really can't thank you enough for suggesting the matchmaking idea. It's genius."

"Don't mention it. You're helping me too, so it's a win-win situation. I can't keep my guys here forever, and until the house is done I can't give them the attention they deserve. They need more than just visits to feed and walk them. They need a home with someone who loves them and can give them what they need. Just like you said."

He led her to the kennels where Berry, Lou Lou and ET were happily running around the holding area.

As they drew closer, Lucy thought she could hear the faint sound of yelping.

"What's that?" she asked. "Did you get puppies?"

"Found them on my way back from work earlier. A box left on the side of the highway on my way back from McKinley. "Akitas."

"Someone just left them on the road to die?" Lucy exclaimed, appalled.

"Looks that way. I almost ran over the box. I drove around it, but something told me to stop and take a look."

She had to repress her anger, not at Scott but the culprits. How could anyone do that? It was winter, and yes maybe the dogs had a thick coat of fur but that was no excuse. It was *cruel.*

She refocused her thoughts. "So, we have some more recruits for our new enterprise."

He bit his lip. "Looks that way. Sorry."

"Don't be. Just makes me even more determined to get this right."

’ ’ ’

Lucy and Scott played with the dogs a little, before taking them out all for a walk and run around the woods before darkness fell.

It gave her a chance to really get to know them.

ET was the most excitable. Lou Lou sniffed around a lot; Lucy could tell she wanted to be out on the hunt.

She was otherwise content, but she wasn't going to be happy being trapped behind a fence for long. She needed more space and attention.

Berry was perfectly happy though. He had space, shelter, the open woods and two very familiar faces. Plus, he was getting all the food he wanted. He was in heaven.

The abandoned Akitas were a different story. Their fur was dirty and they were thin; clear signs of neglect.

A few more days with good food and some loving care and attention would perk them right back up though.

Now Lucy picked up one of the little furballs. "Does this guy have a name?" she asked Scott, as she cradled the pup who wriggled about as she scratched his stomach.

"I haven't had a chance to name them yet. I figure whoever gets them might want to do so themselves."

"Good point." Lucy nodded determinedly. "OK, let's get you guys all prepped and ready for a brand new life."

CHAPTER 16

They returned to the house; Lucy more eager than ever to get started on working to match all these great dogs with the perfect person.

"What do you think about this?" she asked Scott, a little while later, reciting the profile she'd just created.

She cleared her throat.

"Single, rambunctious three-year-old Kelpie named ET, phoning home. Gentle, peaceable and hard-working. He loves long walks, exercise, chasing balls, discs and playing hide-and-seek. Needs love from someone who is active and involved, and who wants a dog to put to work. Give him a job and he'll give you more than enough love in return."

"Sounds great!" Scott replied, shaking his head in admiration. "I knew you'd be amazing at this."

She smiled, thrilled with the praise. "I'll get right to work on one for Lou Lou."

"Can I make you something?" he asked as he stepped away from the table. "I haven't eaten all day."

She looked distractedly up from her notebook.

"You know, neither have I. Not since lunch anyway. That'd be nice. Thanks."

"You really are doing a great job *and* you're a natural," he commented as he walked over to the cupboards and began to collect items to prepare something.

Lucy wasn't used to hearing so much praise and she wasn't sure how to respond to it. She never did anything for recognition really; it was always passion that drove her.

And this time she had a dual reason. She wanted to help the dogs first and foremost, but helping Scott was also very satisfying. He worked hard. He cared. He wanted to do right by these animals, and she was going to see to it that he got his wish.

"I hope you like French food," he said as he began to chop some vegetables.

"Never had it," she confessed.

"Never?"

She shook her head. "I don't really go out much."

"None of your boyfriends ever took you to a French restaurant? That's a travesty."

Lucy began to fidget. "Umm, well, I never really had that many boyfriends."

"How many have you had?" he asked casually.

She hesitated. What would he think if she told him?

"I don't know if I should answer that."

"Why not? It's just a number."

"Fine. If it's just a number, how many girlfriends have you had?" she retorted.

"Three," he replied nonchalantly.

"That's all?" Lucy was surprised.

He smirked. "Yup. I was fifteen when I started out with Linda. We were together for three years. Broke up because of college. Susan and I got together my junior year of college and were together for six. Then I met Hailey when I was twenty-six or seven and we were together for five. I've been single ever since."

Lucy blinked. She realized she didn't even know how old Scott was. "How old are you?"

"Thirty-three. Why?"

"Nothing," she said with a shake of her head. "Was just asking."

"So I answered your question. Now answer mine."

Discomfited, Lucy took a deep breath and sighed. "One."

"Really? Only one?"

She could hear the disbelief in his voice. "Yep. Just one."

"That's strange. I would've thought you'd be fighting them off," he stated as he continued to chop.

"Why would you think that?" she asked honestly.

"Why wouldn't I?"

Where did he get those eyes from? Whenever Lucy looked directly into them her stomach flipped about, her mind boggled and her tongue got twisted.

He was so much easier to talk to when he wasn't looking right at her.

He wouldn't be single for very long though. She could think of at least three women she knew who would be perfect for him. Tall, beautiful, intelligent and who could actually hold a conversation while making eye-to-eye contact.

"Well?" he urged.

"Well, what?" she replied, coloring.

He turned back to what he was doing. "So why haven't you dated more?"

Lucy leaned forward on her elbows and clasped her hands under her chin. "I've always been … shy," she admitted.

"Painfully so, sometimes. Doesn't really work well when trying to communicate with other people. Especially guys."

"You're shy?" He seemed surprised. "I wouldn't have thought so. You're so happy and chatty in my eyes."

"That's because of the dogs," she admitted. "I'm better with them than people. They don't disappoint."

"Ah OK. So, someone disappointed you," he stated perceptively.

"I guess you could say that. My dad walked out on my mom when I was eleven. She died a year later and I got sent to live with my Grandma."

Scott stopped to look back at her again. "I'm really sorry to hear that."

"It's okay. It was a long time ago." She sighed. "I started seeing a guy when I was eighteen, but he was just playing with me. I thought he was serious. I guess I didn't know any better at the time."

"He was an idiot," Scott said with feeling. "Anyone who wouldn't take someone like you seriously could only be one."

When she looked up, he was still watching her, those eyes boring into her gaze.

But this time Lucy didn't blush. She simply smiled. "Thank you."

CHAPTER 17

❄

Visitors from all around the area flocked to Whitedale for this year's Holiday Fair and tree lighting ceremony.

Grant Square was the center of Whitedale; a large roundabout with a grassy middle, it was the heart of the town. And at Christmas, it was the yuletide epicenter.

White and colored strings of twinkling lights crisscrossed the square from one corner to another. Large wreaths decorated with white lights, red ribbon, and pinecones hung at the entrance from every access point.

The tree itself, erected at the center and surrounded by decorative gift boxes, was the final touch.

The official lighting ceremony occurred exactly one week before Christmas every year. Twelve feet of Douglas Fir stood fully adorned in silver, white and royal blue.

There were ribbons, balls, icicles, and the remnants of snowfall from the night before. Even without the lights, it was beautiful.

This evening, the entire town was out in force, and Lucy

was loving the holiday atmosphere.

For her 12 Dogs of Christmas matchmaking booth, Mary had given her a spot close to the Christmas tree to maximize foot traffic.

Now, standing at the booth surrounded by festive profile photos and cute bios for the dogs, it was the first time since her grandmother's death that she remembered being happy at this time of year.

"Hey Lucy," Mary called out, as she approached her with a smile. "Merry Christmas."

"Same to you. Great turn out," she commented.

The other woman looked gleeful. "Isn't it? I think it's the best we've had since I became head of the committee."

"You're doing a great job," Lucy stated as she rearranged some of the profiles out front.

Mary smiled at the presentation. "This looks great. How has the response been so far?"

Lucy beamed. It was like the sun was inside of her trying to get out. "Amazing actually," she told her. "I already have a dozen or so prospective families. I'll vet them over the next few days and hopefully have these pups cosy in their new homes in time for Christmas."

She couldn't believe the response already. So many potential families! She was sure that among them was the perfect home for each of her and Scott's furry friends.

"Keep it up," Mary encouraged. "I've got to go. It's almost showtime."

"Hey there," Scott called out then, approaching.

"You brought them!" Lucy exclaimed happily, realizing he had Lou Lou, ET, and Berry with him; their tails wagging merrily when they saw her.

"I couldn't leave these guys home, especially today. The

perfect real-life canine additions."

He got closer and smiled at the display. "Wow, you really did a great job with this. It looks spectacular." He picked up the flier for Rex and Roza, a couple of Border Collies he'd found in Gafferton. Their owner didn't want them and was going to put them down if no one took them, so Scott did.

"Tenacious twins Rex and Roza, six-month-old Border Collies, are looking for an active owner," he read aloud. "Energetic, intelligent, agile and balanced; they need a home where they can have lots to do. Perfect for farmers and an ideal work dog, these pooches love a cuddle after the workday is done. Both means double the love."

Lucy smiled. "Like it?"

He grinned. "It's perfect. Did you have any takers?"

Lucy grabbed the sign-up sheet and held it out to him in giddy triumph. "Four already for these two alone."

"I knew you could do it," he encouraged, as the dogs milled around, sniffing the foreign scents filling the square.

"I haven't done it *yet*," she reminded him, trying to rein in both their enthusiasm. But she couldn't deny she was very hopeful.

"You will. I'm sure of it." Scott smiled. "Have you had a chance to look around the other stalls yet?"

"Not really. It's been so busy already. Oh hello big guy," Berry came up her, his huge tale almost levelling the booth, and she reached down and scratched him round the ears.

Lucy was so completely dedicated to her task she sometimes got tunnel vision. Today was one such occasion. She really wanted to find these animals a home and that had been her foremost thought. Especially when it came to Berry.

She'd already talked to some people who were potentially great matches and hoped his new owner was amongst them.

She also hoped it would be someone in, or close to town so that she could keep walking him.

She'd miss him if he wound up in a different county where she couldn't see him anymore. She couldn't be selfish, however. If the perfect home for Berry was far away, then she'd have no choice but to say goodbye.

"Well, why don't we grab a quick bite and take a look around before the ceremony starts?"

Now, Lucy looked at the big, happy dog as he wandered around the area, glancing curiously at the lights and festivity.

No, she couldn't imagine not seeing him every day. It would be a hard thing to get used to.

"Lucy?"

Her eyes snapped up at the sound of Scott's voice, and she realized she hadn't replied. "Sorry. Yes, good idea.I was just thinking."

"About Berry?"

She nodded. "I just realized that I'm really going to miss him."

He looked at her thoughtfully. "I think maybe you should cross that bridge when you come to it."

"You're right. No sense crying over spilled milk when the carton's still in the fridge."

Scott chuckled. "A ... different take on it but yes, I guess."

"I'm a bit corny," she admitted, embarrassed. "My Grandma always said if it was something out of the way and a little bit odd, I'd probably say it."

"I think I would've very much liked to have met your grandmother," Scott stated and she smiled, realizing that Grandma in turn would have liked him a lot too.

Now he held out his arm to her. "Shall we?"

She smiled hooking it. "Let's."

CHAPTER 18

❄

The lighting ceremony was spectacular.

The children's choir sang *Silent Night* beautifully, before Mary made her introduction to the Mayor, who duly flipped the switch and lit up the massive fir in beautiful, twinkling splendour.

Lucy and Scott watched it all as they stood side-by-side with steaming hot chocolate in hand, the dogs between them.

Scott lingered on at the booth a little after the ceremony, and when the time came for the fair to close, he stepped behind the scenes to help tidy-up, settling the dogs by a lamppost nearby.

Lucy smiled at his gallantry. "Thanks."

"My pleasure." He began to collect the fliers and place them into one of the boxes she had stored underneath the countertop.

"You know, Berry really seems to like it a lot at your house," she commented, as she cleaned up. "And tonight, he behaved like a dream in your presence. Have you ever thought of taking him in yourself?"

Scott paused a little, and all of sudden Lucy worried that she'd overstepped.

He sighed. "Berry is a great dog. We both know that. I just think that maybe there's someone else out there who'd be a better person for him."

"Really, who?" she asked, intrigued. If Scott had an idea of someone in particular then she wanted to know.

He smiled a little. "I can't say yet. I just know that I'm not the right one, sorry." He stepped closer then, and Lucy's stomach fluttered as he gently brushed a stray tendril of hair behind her ear, as if by way of apology.

She sighed and bent down to pick up a box, now feeling bad to have assumed.

"You're right, I was just reaching, and I met some really good prospects today already. It's just … I really don't want to have to send him away."

"I know. But when the time comes, I know you'll do what's best for him. So, all done?" he asked as he stacked up the final box.

"I think so." All of a sudden she felt exhausted. "Man I'm beat."

"You're like me," Scott chuckled. "Once I get my teeth into something I can't stop until it's done. I'll skip meals and even showers."

Her face wrinkled. "That's gross."

"No, that's manual labor. When I want to get work done on the house I get up, put on some clothes and get to it. I can shower before bed. I just need to get going."

"I hope you don't plan to do that when you find your next girlfriend," she commented. "I'm sure she wouldn't find you nearly as appealing."

"Trust me, if I had a girlfriend, there would be a lot of different things in my life."

She turned to look at him, wondering what he meant. What would he even need to change?

"So - see you tomorrow?" Scott enquired, as he closed the door of Lucy's truck once they'd got everything back inside.

"I could maybe stop by after I finish following up with some of the families. We could discuss the options? I've got a lot to get through over the next few days."

"Great. I can make you dinner and you can see Berry of course," he added with a grin.

"Sounds great to me. See you then," Lucy turned her key in the ignition, and glanced back at the twinkling Christmas tree, the backdrop to a waving Scott and his waggy-tailed companions.

And as she drove away, she couldn't help but smile.

Despite her tiredness, tonight had been the nicest time she'd spent in ages.

CHAPTER 19

❄

Days passed and Lucy went about her dog-walking duties as normal, but as soon as she dropped her charges back, off she went to visit prospective owners for the rescues.

The very first day, she found a home for two of the Akita puppies, and was over the moon when she went to Scott's that evening to share the news and see Berry.

Day after day, the process went pretty much the same. She walked her dogs as usual, then afterward visited prospective owners before meeting up with Scott and Berry.

Some days she had good news to share and others, she just went to see Berry, enjoy Scott's company - and not having to go home to an empty apartment.

"I really think ET's going to be so happy," she told Scott now, excited to have found a match for his rescue pup. "Joseph Steinbeck is perfect for him. He's a fireman and trains every day, so taking ET for walks and getting him exercise won't be a problem. Plus, he said they're looking at adding more dogs to the rescue team and ET would be ideal for that.

Yes, he's a bit on the older side to start training, but from what I've observed he's very compliant and with the right trainer and some patience, could make a really great rescue dog."

"You're really excited about this," Scott mused as he brought a platter of pizza over to the couch.

Drinks were already on the coffee table and Lucy was curled up on the couch with the remote in her hand surfing Netflix for a movie.

"Aren't you?"

"Of course. And I knew you'd be great at all this, I just never thought it would all happen so quickly. You know, I think we really are going to get all these guys re-homed in time for Christmas."

"Of course we are," Lucy said satisfied. "Once I make a plan I execute it."

"Good to know."

Scott settled on the couch beside her. Lucy wasn't sure what she was in the mood to watch tonight. TV could be a wasteland; you could get lost and never actually find that one thing you really wanted to watch. It was the ultimate 'too much choice' dilemma.

"Having trouble deciding?" he asked as she continued to skim through titles.

"I don't know what I feel like tonight," she admitted. "You pick."

He took the remote from her as Lucy pulled out a slice of meat lover's pizza. Scott had doubled every topping, making it the most loaded pizza she'd ever seen.

When she looked back at the screen, she laughed out loud at the title he'd highlighted.

"OK. *Lassie* it is."

CHAPTER 20

It was now only three days til Christmas and Lucy was still on the hunt for a home for Berry.

Lou Lou, ET and the Akitas were gone. A farmer named Jasper Tucker had taken Lou Lou. He liked to go on frequent hunting trips, was in his thirties and active. He was perfect for a Coonhound.

Now, she was personally delivering Rex and Roza to their new owners.

"Now, dogs are fun, but a really big responsibility," she informed the Dickersons' two small children.

"Can I ride on their backs?" four-year-old Billy asked. "I saw it on TV."

Lucy smiled indulgently. "That's actually not so good for the dogs. They weren't built to bear weight on their backs like that. You could hurt them."

"Then why did they do it on TV?" Five-year-old Sydney wanted to know.

Their parents smiled. "They're just curious," their mother commented.

"That's good, means they're interested," Lucy replied. She turned back to the children. "They probably didn't know better, but you do now, so you can take even better care of your new furry friends. That's what you want, right?"

The children chorused a happy yes.

"Now Rex and Roza aren't like your toys, OK? You have to help your mom and dad take care of them." The children were too young to take care of the dogs on their own, but it was good to have them help so that one day they could take more responsibility.

Good pet ownership started when kids were small, Lucy believed. Not that she thought they'd have any trouble here. The Dickersons owned a ranch, and animals were everywhere.

Rex and Roza would have work to do once they were older, but for now, they were a great addition to the family.

Lucy left the children to play with their new pets while she turned her focus to the ones who'd really be taking care of the dogs, their parents.

"So I know we went through everything before, but I just wanted to emphasize a few things. When it comes to their diet, make sure you watch them carefully. They do a lot of exercising, but you have to be wary of overfeeding them. Treats will help you to train them, but too many can affect their weight. Here are a few."

She handed over the bag of treats she usually bought for her charges. "You'll want to use a pin brush once or twice a week to keep their coat free of mats, tangles, and debris. You'll need to do that more frequently during shedding season."

"Shedding season?" Lynda Dickerson asked.

"Yes. It gets pretty hairy then," Lucy mused ruefully. "But you'll be fine. You're just going to need to brush them more.

You can make it something fun for the kids to do. Speaking of the children … collies tend to want to lead those smaller than them, animals and children. Your two are a bit older, and you've said they're well-behaved so that shouldn't be a problem, but I'd still keep an eye on them just for the initial phase, as both the kids and the dogs adjust."

"Thank you," James said. "We've had dogs before but we've never had anyone do what you've done in making sure we got the right animals for our family, and for our family's needs. Plus, you really seem to care about the well-being of these animals. There should be more like you."

Lucy could feel her cheeks getting hot with the compliment. She wasn't used to them and it only made her social discomfort even more apparent.

Still, she couldn't deny that all of this was making her feel good.

"Thank you."

BUT AT THIS POINT, everyone had a home but Berry.

Lucy had met with several families who were interested in having the big dog as an addition to their family. They'd made it on to her list, so they had the basic requirements, but once she met them was when she saw the faults.

"I'm sorry Mr. Chase, I just don't think Berry would fit here," Lucy stated as she sat in the living room of Simon Chase's house.

"Why not?" he asked. "I have space outside and I can afford the cost of his care."

"Yes, that's true," she replied. "But he doesn't like staying outside all the time. His previous owner, Mrs. Cole, kept him exclusively in the house at night. Your house is a great size, but you have a lot of stuff in here and I can tell some of it is expensive. Outside just wouldn't work with Berry. He likes to be where the family is and he can't do that in here."

Simon nodded. "It wouldn't matter to me much. I'm sure I could get it done. Maybe move a few things around?"

"You could try, but it might just make you and Berry uncomfortable. Truthfully, I think another type of dog would suit you best."

"I see. Thank you for your honesty," Simon said as he extended his hand to her.

"I'm really sorry to disappoint you," she continued as she got to her feet and took his hand.

"It's quite alright. Thanks for coming out."

But as Lucy left yet another fruitless prospective match for Berry, she had to wonder if maybe the ultimate fault lay with her.

CHAPTER 21

She ambled back to her truck, unable to shake the thought.

Simon Chase would've been a great match for Berry, albeit not for the inside of his house.

What was she saying? She could've let it slide and let him have Berry. Did it really matter that he wouldn't be living the same way he did with Mrs. Cole? He was out of the house a lot with Scott now as it was.

And if Simon Chase was willing to risk his property, who was she to say otherwise?

"You have to stop being so particular," she told herself as she got back into the vehicle. She sat behind the wheel and stared out at the slowly falling snow.

Berry was special to her though. She wanted him to have the perfect situation.

OK, so her apartment was small, and obviously her landlord wouldn't let her have a dog, but Lucy couldn't help but think that he still would've been happiest of all with her.

She certainly would've felt better. She wouldn't need to

worry about him. She could take care of him just the way Mrs. Cole would've wanted.

She could do it.

So maybe she should think about getting a different apartment?

It could work, she realized excitedly. She could look for someplace else to live. Someplace big enough for her and Berry, with a landlord who didn't mind pets.

Lucy started the truck. She'd bounce the idea off Scott and see what he thought.

"I THINK IT'S ME," she sighed, when later, she flopped down at a chair around Scott's makeshift kitchen table.

"What is?" he asked, as poured kibble into a bowl for Berry.

"Not being able to find a home for this big guy. Maybe I'm too picky."

"Not necessarily. You just know Berry so well and who'd be right for him. Look what you did for my rescues. Every last one of them has the perfect home now, and that was all you."

"So why not Berry then? Why is it so hard?"

"I don't know," he said. "Why don't you tell me?"

"I was thinking about it while I was leaving the Chase house. Maybe I keep finding faults in every prospective pet owner, because deep down inside I don't believe anyone would take care of Berry as well as I would," she admitted.

Scott turned to her with raised eyebrows. "Keep going."

"You aren't going to say anything?"

"Not right now. I'd rather hear where else you're going with this."

"Well," she said, continuing. "I know I don't have the

perfect place to keep him right now. My apartment is small, but I could change that. I could get a new place. It might take a while, but I could do it."

"What would you do with him until then?"

She grimaced a little. "I was kinda hoping I could leave him here with you, if you'd let me?" she asked hopefully. "It wouldn't be for long. I hope. Just until I found a bigger place that would suit both of us."

"A different apartment?"

"No other choice. Besides, it's not as though he'd be home alone when I'm working, because I'd take him on all the walks with me as normal."

"True."

Scott put the dog food away and handed Lucy the bowl. They walked to the holding area together where Berry was running around the enclosure and came bounding up to the gate the second he saw them.

Lucy smiled, she would never get tired of the sight of him running towards her, his large ears flopping on either side of his head, tongue hanging out as if he was smiling.

They opened the gate and stepped inside. Lucy walked to the kennel, but Berry was already trying to get his head into the bowl.

"Hold on a minute," she giggled as she gently pushed his head away and set the food down. Berry bounded over and dove right in the second she stepped away.

She stood staring at the big dog with her hands stuffed in her pockets, then looked at Scott. "I'm being silly, aren't I?"

"Why would you say that?" he asked.

"To think I could honestly do a better job taking care of him than people who have the space, and are willing to compromise their lifestyle to have him." She sighed heavily.

Scott's hand moved to rest gently on her shoulder. "I don't think so."

Lucy turned to look at him, surprised. "Really?"

"Really."

"So you think this could be the right thing?" she asked, hopeful.

"I think you've finally realized what I've known all along," he said gently and turned her to face him. His hands were on her arms, holding her gently. "Lucy, you *are* his perfect person."

She couldn't describe what it felt like when she heard those words come out of Scott's mouth. Deep down inside she'd always known she didn't want a dog *like* Berry. She wanted *him*. She wanted the big guy as her pet, her trusty companion, but was content to just help Mrs. Cole.

Then, the more time she got to spend with him, the more she realized how great it was to have him with her all the time.

"Thanks for that," she told Scott as she smiled up at him.

"For what?"

"For saying that. I needed to hear it."

"Why?"

"I guess I needed to know someone else besides me thought it was a good fit," she admitted bashfully. "I may not have everything he needs right now, but ..." She shrugged.

"I agree. Sometimes you don't have to have everything perfect though, Lucy. Sometimes you just have to have the heart. That's enough for now. The rest will come. And you have the heart," he continued. "I've known that for ages. It's why I wanted to meet you."

His confession took her by surprise. "You - meet me?

"Yes, Mrs. Cole told me about this wonderful woman who came to walk Berry," he chuckled. "She raved about you."

The sentiment made Lucy's heart sing. She'd never told Mrs. Cole how highly she regarded her, so it was nice to know that the older woman felt the same way about her.

"That day we met was purely coincidental, but the second I saw you running behind Berry, I know you were the best person for both of them," Scott continued. "Mrs. Cole needed someone to help, and Berry needed someone who could give him what she no longer could."

Lucy was beaming now.

"Since then I've watched you go all out for him. Persuading people to take care of him. Trying to find a home day after day. You were relentless, and the person who loved him enough to do all of that could only be the best one for him." He looked directly at her, those eyes boring into her gaze again. "You're the perfect match, Lucy. I've just been waiting for you to realize it."

CHAPTER 22

Lucy hadn't really been able to enjoy Christmas since her grandmother's death.

But this would be the first time in years that she wasn't going to spend the day alone.

Instead, Scott had asked her over. She brought a homemade pecan pie with her and a bottle of mulled wine that she'd bought at the fair.

He was waiting on the porch when she arrived; Berry beside him. The big dog ran to her the second she got out of the truck, and immediately tried to stick his big head in the pie.

"Oh no you don't," she chided gently. "This isn't for you."

The dog snorted and walked away.

"For the first time ever, I think you disappointed him," Scott commented as he leaned against the post watching her. She had a red wool hat on her head and a cosy matching peacoat.

The snow that morning was heavy and the wind icy in every direction.

"Aren't you cold?" she asked him as she approached the entryway. Though he was wearing a cosy sweater that looked like it could be cashmere.

Having only ever seen him in work shirts and jeans, it was a nice change.

"I have the heating on," he said with a smile. "Besides, I wasn't out here long. Berry let me know you were on your way."

"He must've heard the truck coming down the road," Lucy mused as she stepped inside.

However, the sound of another vehicle approach from behind drew her attention and she turned back to see two cars and another truck making their way up the driveway. "Who's that?" she asked a little unnerved.

"Just a few of my friends," Scott said casually.

"Your friends?" Lucy almost shrieked. She'd come over today thinking it was just the two of them, a casual thing as always. She wasn't ready to meet strangers.

"Don't be scared," he chuckled, reading her mind. "They won't bite. I promise."

"Why didn't you tell me though?"

"I didn't actually know they were coming until this morning. They wanted to surprise me and drove all the way here from Denver. I couldn't tell them no." He gave her a big smile and then took the pie from her hands. Why did he have to smile like that? It made Lucy forget about her shyness. "Besides, I wanted them to meet you," he added mysteriously.

"Me...why?"

"Is there something wrong with wanting my oldest friends to meet one of my newest?" he responded.

"What if they don't like me? You know I'm not great with strangers."

"Who is?" He shook his head. "It doesn't matter anyway. I've already told them all about you."

Lucy's eyes widened. "What did you tell them?"

"Just that I met this crazy woman who loves dogs and smiles like sunshine," he commented offhandedly.

Her heart fluttered, but she dismissed it with a scoff.

"So you made me sound way better than I am."

"I don't exaggerate, Lucy. If I say you're wonderful, it's because you are."

Then, before she could react, Scott winked and hopped down off the porch to greet his friends.

CHAPTER 23

✻

"Merry Christmas!" a cheerful female voice called out.

It belonged to a lithe blonde. She ran to Scott, threw her arms around his neck and smacked his cheek with a kiss. "You big lug. How've you been?" But didn't give him a chance to reply before she turned to Lucy. "And you must be Lucy. So nice to meet you finally," she said moving to embrace her too.

Finally...? Lucy was completely off-guard but did her best to return the welcoming gesture.

"Ted, could you get those things in here pronto?" the woman asked, turning to a man getting stuff out of the car behind her. "Kids, come on in out of the cold." She looked to Scott again. "Where's the bathroom these days?"

"Through there, just past the kitchen," he indicated with a roll of his eyes. "Same as last time."

"I'll drop this off on the way," She grabbed the pie from Scott's hands and hurried on her way.

Lucy watched her go. "Who was that?" she laughed.

"That whirlwind is Roxanna. I've known her since I was in

high school. She's a bundle of energy and the friendliest person you'll ever meet."

"Uncle Scott!" a chorus sounded as three children, two girls and a boy came running in their direction.

"Hey, here comes trouble!" Scott declared as he stooped to hug them.

"We missed you, Uncle Scott," said the oldest girl. She was blonde like her mother and cute as a button.

"Me or my hot chocolate?"

"The chocolate," they answered in unison, and Lucy had to smile.

"At least you're honest," Scott turned to introduce her. "This is Lucy. And this is Jennifer, Morgan, and Tyler."

"Hi!" they all chorused together. They were adorable and he was adorable with them.

"Hey kids," she answered with a small wave. "Merry Christmas."

"Get inside and take your jackets off. The TV's that way," he added and they scampered off immediately.

"And this is Roxy's husband Ted," Scott supplied, as a tall, slightly balding man approached the house.

"Don't tell me. Lucy," he commented with a smile. "I'd give you a hug but as you can see I'm the bag man for this trip."

She laughed. "Would you like some help?"

"Love some to be honest."

"I can get it," Scott interjected.

"No, you have more guests to greet. I can help," Lucy insisted as she grabbed a few of the packages Ted had in his arms.

Soon the other guests arrived. Anita and Paul, two of Scott's friends from Ireland who were staying with Bryan and his sister Lydia in Denver, and had chosen to tag along when they heard of their impromptu plan to surprise him.

They had come prepared too. They brought turkey and stuffing, sweet potato pie, macaroni and cheese, salads, garlic bread, and wine.

Along with the roast ham, potatoes, candied yams, green beans and pumpkin soup Scott had already prepared, they had a true Christmas feast to look forward to.

THE FOOD LASTED ALL the way through the afternoon, with Ted then whipping out some beers.

The men set up in front of the TV, while the women chatted in the kitchen and the kids preoccupied themselves with the gifts their parents had brought, but mostly with Berry.

The big dog was a huge hit amongst the guests.

They each took turns scratching behind his ears and commenting on how amicable he was, surprised that a dog that big could be so gentle and easy with children.

"So Lucy, we've all heard tons about you, and now that it's just us girls here," Roxy grinned, indicated the guys who were enthralled in a game on TV. "What's the deal with you two?"

She looked up in slight alarm. "Me and Scott?"

"Yes," the other woman pressed. "Spill."

They were standing around the kitchen island staring at her, as Lydia washed the dishes and Lucy dried.

Roxy was responsible for packing them away.

"Oh yes, do tell," Lydia urged. "We promise not to say a word." She grinned and continued to scrub the remnants of the turkey roast from the pan.

"Well, Scott's my friend obviously. He's … nice," Lucy replied nervously.

She hated being put on the spot at the best of times, but this was even worse. They were questioning her relationship with Scott and she wasn't entirely sure what that was. They'd become so close this last while, but that was it. Wasn't it?

"That's it?" Anita scoffed. "Please, anyone can tell that guy is falling *hard*."

"You think so?" Lucy questioned uncertainly.

"Definitely," Roxy agreed. "When a guy talks about a woman as much as he talks about you, there has to be more to it than he's saying."

"So he said something to you?"

"Of course not," Lydia replied with a roll of her eyes. "He denies there's anything, just like you're doing," she grinned. "Thing is I don't believe either of you."

"Don't believe what?" Scott's voice interjected suddenly.

"That there's nothing between you and Lucy, that's what," Roxy stated.

"What's between him and Lucy?" Bryan asked, going to the fridge for another beer.

Scott looked at Lucy and she looked back at him, her cheeks reddening.

"See, look at them," Roxy reiterated. "Why don't you two stop playing coy and just admit it?"

"Rox …" her husband warned.

Scott cleared his throat. "If there was something to say…"

"… then we would," Lucy put in quickly.

Lydia chuckled. "They're even finishing each other's sentences already."

"Definitely something there," Bryan teased.

"Why are you all so eager to make Lucy and I into something?" Scott asked nonchalantly.

"Because it's painfully obvious there *is* something," Roxanna tut-tutted. "We'd all like to see you happy, and I'm sure I speak for everyone when I say that from what we've heard and seen today, we all give you two a big thumbs up."

Despite herself, Lucy smiled brightly. "You guys are great too," she said.

"See! Perfect! She fits naturally into our ragtag bunch," Roxanna continued as she draped an arm around Lucy's neck. She looked at Scott. "So why not just come right out and say it?"

"Rox, if I had something to say, I assure you it would not be public," Scott replied firmly. "And when I do have something to say, Lucy will be the first to hear it."

His gaze met hers as she spoke and she found her breath catch in her lungs. This was incredibly … awkward.

What did he mean?

"Forgive my wife," Ted demurred, as he came over and hugged Roxanna from behind. "Once she gets something into her head, she doesn't let go."

"Got that right. That's how I snagged you." Roxanna planted a light kiss on his lips, and they all laughed.

"Way to change the subject," Bryan commented with a chuckle. "Now is there anymore beer …"

CHAPTER 24

It was after eight that evening when the group decided that it was time to leave. It was starting to snow again, and they needed to get going if they wanted to make it back to the city before the worst of it.

Lucy and Scott stood on the porch and waved goodbye. He draped his arm lightly around her shoulders and she leaned against him as the snow fell gently all around.

It was the kind of warm, cosy, *homely* holiday moment she'd only ever seen on TV.

And she couldn't believe it was real.

This Christmas had yielded more than she could ever expect. Not only did she have a new friend, but friends plural.

And lately with Scott, a real sense of companionship; something that she'd been missing for far too long.

"So, what do you think? Not a complete disaster, right?" he asked as he closed the door behind them.

"I think they're wonderful," she admitted. "I really liked them all and the kids are so sweet."

"So I hope you're not going to leave me now too?" he asked, as he turned to her.

The cars were almost out of sight.

She shook her head. She'd just had the nicest Christmas Day ever and she didn't want it to end just yet. "Why do good things always go by so quickly though?"

"So we can have more of them," Scott shivered. "Let's get back inside out of this cold. Feel like some hot chocolate?" he suggested, leading back inside.

"I'd love some. Though I truly didn't think I could fit in anything else after all that food."

The kitchen was immaculate now, with little to no remnants of the humongous feast that had been enjoyed earlier that day.

"Go find a movie. I'll bring the chocolate," Scott stated as he began pulling out ingredients.

Lucy wandered into the living room.

Berry was nestled by the fireplace snoozing contentedly, and she had to smile.

Like it or not, the big dog had pretty much already made this house his home.

Scott came in a few minutes later with two steaming cups of his famous homemade hot chocolate. His was plain but there were marshmallows on hers, just as she liked it.

He stretched out on the couch and Lucy adjusted herself on the opposite end, with her feet towards him.

"*It's a Wonderful Life* is on. Do you want to watch it?" It was her all time favorite Christmas movie. She could never get over James Stewart's characterization of George Bailey.

Scott smiled. "I love that movie. My Mom liked to watch it every Christmas," he informed her.

They settled down to watch the movie, while the fire

crackled lightly beneath the TV screen, Berry asleep beneath it.

Lucy sipped at the warm beverage, feeling more content and cosy than she'd ever been in her entire life.

Scott tugged at her toes and she giggled.

"Merry Christmas Lucy."

She smiled. "Merry Christmas."

THEY MUST'VE FALLEN asleep watching the movie, because when Lucy was awakened by Berry's damp tongue licking her face, the sun was just coming up over the horizon.

Across the way, Scott was still asleep, now hugging a cushion to his chest.

She couldn't help but watch him as he slept so peacefully, properly studying the contours of his face without having to worry about him catching her.

Berry nudged her again.

"Alright, I get it. You're hungry," she whispered.

She eased herself from the couch and padded into the kitchen. She got his bowl and the dog food and fixed him his breakfast.

Then she had an idea. Scott had cooked for her so many times already; why didn't she do something from him today?

Lucy set to work at making breakfast. She knew where most things were, having watched him prepare stuff for her so many times.

Soon, she had everything she needed to make them something delicious.

He kept a well-stocked pantry and everything was there to make sweet crepes, sausages, eggs and biscuits.

It had been a while since she'd had a reason to make a big

meal like this, and wouldn't bother for just herself, but for Scott it was no trouble.

The smell must have awakened him because he walked into the room just as Lucy was plating the eggs.

"Morning," she greeted cheerfully.

"Good morning," he replied with a grin. "What's all this?"

"This is what I like to call breakfast," she replied. "Have a seat." She brought the plates and cutlery to the table, along with the pot of coffee she'd brewed. "Bon appétit."

They talked and laughed and ate. She couldn't remember ever feeling so at ease with anyone.

Scott was special, that was clear, but the problem was the more Lucy spent time with him and the more they shared, the more she realized she wanted.

CHAPTER 25

Scott cleaned up after, protesting that the cook didn't clean where he was from.

Lucy appreciated the sentiment, but she was happy to do it, after all it was his house and she'd made the mess.

But he wasn't hearing of it.

Berry began to bark at the door. He'd been pacing back-and-forth for a few minutes.

"I think he wants a walk," Lucy said.

"Let's take him then. I'll get our jackets."

He returned a few minutes later with both of their jackets and helped her slip hers on.

Berry was already gone, bounding off into the woods ahead of them.

She laughed as she watched the big happy dog running around in the snow chasing his tail.

"Look at him," she said with a chuckle. "He just loves it here."

"He does. It's really good having him here too," Scott replied. "How do you like it?"

"What're you talking about? You know I *love* this place. It's amazing," Lucy gasped. "The kind of house anyone would be excited to come home to."

"That's why I chose this spot. I used to love coming here to fish as a kid, so when I heard that it was up for sale I had to grab it."

"Good thing. If I could afford a place like this I would too. It's perfect for dogs and to relax amongst nature. The human company isn't so bad either," she teased with a smile.

"I could say the same about you."

Scott was looking directly at her now, and Lucy's heart was beating faster. "Your friends seem to think there's something more," she said boldly, surprising herself by being so direct.

But she needed to know.

"Do you think there is?" he asked, as they ambled out onto the wooden pier.

The sun was now peeking up just over the mountains.

"I don't know. Is there?" Lucy's heart was beating so fast, she didn't know how she got the words out.

She caught sight of Berry out of the corner of her eye and her heart steadied again as it always did.

He was occupied looking down at his reflection. He loved to look at himself. Mirrors, water, you name it. The big guy loved his own image.

"What do *you* think?" Scott repeated, still not answering her question.

His eyes were still locked on her face.

Lucy sucked in a breath. It was now or never.

"There is for me. What I want to know is -"

She didn't get to finish her sentence. The second the words left her mouth Scott had closed the space between them.

It was so quick that Lucy hadn't a chance to think about what to do before his lips pressed against hers, and her body was pulled flush against him.

Thankfully, she didn't need to think.

What she was feeling was enough. Her senses were reeling, but her fingers still worked. They curled into the lapels of Scott's jacket and held him. It wasn't enough though. A moment later her hands slipped up from his chest and encircled his neck.

His lips moved over hers like silk over skin.

When they finally parted, she was breathless. It took her several seconds to open her eyes. She didn't want to break the spell she was under, but she had to. She had to look at him.

"I've wanted to do that for a long time," he confessed. "I was waiting."

"I'm glad you didn't wait any longer." She chuckled. "I guess Roxy was right."

Scott laughed. "She's always right."

"I'm glad," Lucy stepped toward him again. She raised her chin and pressed her lips to his lightly. "I think I wanted to do that for a long time too."

"Why didn't you?"

The fact that they were having this conversation at all, was still something Lucy was trying to process.

It was made difficult with him looking at her as if she was the most beautiful person he'd ever seen. She'd only ever seen that look in movies. Never directed at her.

"I didn't realize it before," she admitted. "I thought we were just friends. The only thing between us was our love of dogs," she continued. "The jittery feeling in my stomach whenever I was around you was just because of my shyness, I told myself."

"But it wasn't?"

"No," she replied with a small shake of her head, amazed at her own certainty and the fact that she was confident about admitting all this to him. "It was telling me what I hadn't figured out yet."

"I'm just glad we both got the same feeling."

"You know, this stuff doesn't happen to people like me," Lucy laughed softly, and tucked her hair behind her ear.

"People don't fall in love where you're from?" he teased.

Her eyes must've looked like saucers.

"What did you say?"

He smiled. "I said I've fallen in love with you Lucy Adams."

Her face lit up at the words. She could feel the heat radiating from her cheeks as she grinned at him.

CHAPTER 26

Lucy hadn't truly realized she'd fallen for Scott.

It was all so subtle, like the mist rolling in on the surface of a lake. It crept in and before she knew it the house of her heart was entirely filled with it. Pillar to post. Roof to basement.

"I think ... I love you too," she whispered.

He reached for her hand and pulled her gently to him. She fell against him, her hands flat against his chest.

"You know, watching you blush just makes me smile because I know you aren't a woman who pretends. You call it shyness, but actually I think it's just wearing your heart on your sleeve. I can trust that. I can trust you."

"Scott…"

"Listen. I told myself I wasn't taking another chance on a woman. I'd sworn off romance long before I met you. Even after Mrs. Cole told me about you, I just wanted to meet the person who had come to mean so much to her. Then we met. The minute I saw your smile, I knew there was something about you."

She laughed. "All I thought was that you were the cutest construction worker I'd ever seen."

He laughed. "Thanks."

"I didn't think we'd see each other again after that. I was glad when we did," she admitted. "Berry coming across your house that day saved me."

"Saved us both you mean. After that, when I took Berry in and you started visiting him here, I realized that I wanted more. I wanted a relationship, someone I could come home to and drink my mother's hot chocolate with on cold evenings. Someone who would curl up with me on Christmas night by the fire, while the dog slept on the rug."

"I think we've already covered that bit," she chuckled.

"Yeah, we did, and we weren't even trying," Scott answered. "It just happened naturally, like everything else with you and me."

"And I liked coming here," she admitted after a moment. "I liked driving out here and being welcomed. I liked watching you cook," she said with a smile. "That was a surprise."

"And I like cooking for you."

"I've never felt so comfortable around a guy before," Lucy admitted. "Usually, I can't put two words together, but with you, any nervousness just sort of melted away. One second, I couldn't think straight when you were near, the next I found I didn't want to stop talking to you."

"Feeling's mutual, believe me."

Her skin felt as if a gentle electric current was moving over it. The hairs on her arms stood on end and she shivered.

"Lucy?"

"Yes?"

"I'm going to kiss you again if you don't stop me," he declared.

She smiled brightly. "So what's stopping you?"

He really was the best kisser on the planet.

Tender and warm. His hands were firm but soft against her skin. The cold wind that blew off the water was nothing. She couldn't even feel it. His kiss was dizzying, intoxicating, and she was enjoying every second of it.

Berry must've gotten tired looking at his reflection because a moment later he was back by their side with his head nuzzling at their legs.

He barked low and then trotted around them happily.

"I think he approves," Scott commented.

Lucy looked at the big dog and smiled. "I think so too."

"What do you say about us all getting back indoors and having more of my mom's special hot chocolate?"

"Do you still have marshmallows?" she asked as he took her hand and began to lead her toward the house.

"When I knew you were coming for Christmas I bought two bags when I went to the store."

"I do believe you're getting to know me."

"I look forward to knowing everything about you," Scott replied as he squeezed her hand gently. "The full profile. But we don't need one of your matchmaking cards this time. I want to take my own time."

Lucy liked the sound of that.

Berry trotted up beside them, and she let her fingers rest on his back comfortingly.

"It's nearly finished?" Lucy commented now, as she looked at the house. She hadn't seen it from this angle before, but now she could see that he'd finished the roof above the porch, and a lot more had been done to the far side of the house.

"Just about. I had a lot of motivation lately…"

"Motivation?"

"I thought maybe a certain fellow dog-lover might one day, if things went well …. like to make it her home." He looked hesitantly at Lucy and squeezed her hand as they walked and she couldn't speak for joy. "Only if she wanted to of course," he added quickly. "It even comes equipped with a place for her dog."

Emotion consumed her. She'd always known this house would be the perfect home for Berry.

She'd just never expected it could be the perfect forever home for her too.

She smiled at Scott.

"Sounds to me like a match made in heaven."

From the Author:

Thanks for reading this festive collection - I very much hope you enjoyed it and that you'll tune for upcoming Christmas movie adaptations of all three stories!

Read on for a short excerpt of my brand new full length novel, THE BEAUTIFUL LITTLE THINGS, out now.
Thanks again.

NEW NOW

THE BEAUTIFUL LITTLE THINGS

PROLOGUE

The magic was missing...

Romy Moore sat at the window chair in her late mother's study and looked out over the nearby woods and forestry trails, appreciating why her mum had always found this spot so peaceful.

The trees wore a light dusting of white, the family home's elevated position in the Dublin Mountains ensuring they always got a bit of proper snow in winter, as opposed to the typically damper stuff on lower ground.

Fittingly beautiful for the season, but also serving merely to highlight the fact that everything felt so ... wrong.

Romy's world was so out of kilter now that it should be howling gales and driving rain out, not Christmas-card perfection. It made everything even more desperately hollow and painful, and now she understood why some people found this time of year so difficult. The forced festive gaiety, the crippling sense of nostalgia and the idea that everything was supposed to be so bloody *wonderful*. When all she wanted to do right then was pull the covers over her head like it was just another day, a normal day, and she didn't have to pretend to be OK, to try to cheer up and put a brave face on for anyone else's sake.

And most of all, not to have to lie to herself that this time of year, to say nothing of *life*, could ever be the same without her mother.

Romy turned back to the desk and opened up a drawer, seeking a tissue. She found an already open packet of Kleenex and paused a little, reflecting that her mum would've likely used the one just before it, oblivious to the fact that her youngest would be needing the next to grieve her passing.

She wiped her eyes and then blew her nose into the tissue, looking idly through bits and pieces scattered across the desk before coming across a prettily patterned notebook beneath some letters.

Opening the cover, she saw her mother's familiar neat handwriting swirl into focus, achingly comforting, and as she began to read the opening words on the page, Romy quickly realised it was one of her journals.

Her mother loved to write and had kept a journal for as long as Romy could remember – ever the traditionalist at heart, despite her sister Joanna's grand attempt a couple of years back to move her into the twenty-first century with the gift of an iPad.

Feeling like an interloper for even daring to read – these were her mother's private thoughts, after all – she couldn't help but be drawn in, desperate to feel close to her once more.

If you are reading this, then for certain I am no longer with you.

In body at least.

Indeed, it is hard for me to be writing this now, from a place where I am still full of the joys, having just watched you all depart our very last family Christmas together.

While this year's gathering was, in a word . . . eventful, it gives me such joy that all ended happily – just as I'd hoped.

I wish I could imagine how your lives have been since – and, admittedly, I have tried – but when I attempt to imagine any scenarios that have transpired in the interim, I tend to go down a rabbit hole and overwhelm myself.

I cannot control what will happen. Just as I cannot see the future, I have no way of knowing how any of you will handle my passing.

The only thing I can do from this vantage point right this minute is provide my thoughts, my words, and perhaps a little bit of motherly advice.

I'm trying to picture you all together this time next year without me – and truth be told, I struggle with the concept because it feels so foreign.

So bear with me, as I seek to find the words and comb the recesses of my mind for any wisdom or reminders that might be useful as you navigate the festive period without me.

Firstly, it's OK to feel sad . . . but not forever.

And please do not let grief colour the first Christmas where I am absent. Whatever you do, don't allow sorrow to serve as the backdrop.

Because, oh my darlings, it is still the absolute best time of year and as you know has always been my favourite.

So please, for my sake, celebrate this Christmas as if I was still here?

Because I will be, in my own way – in all the little festive tradi-

tions we have followed over the years, and recipes and rituals that have become our family's staples.

Yes, of course this will be a Christmas like no other.

But that doesn't mean it has to be a terrible one.

It was like . . . a gift, Romy thought, a lump in her throat; though obviously not for her alone.

Because of course her mother would have understood that the family's first holiday period without her would be impossibly difficult.

Though she couldn't possibly have known just how scattered and broken they'd all become since her passing.

But maybe . . . Romy thought, sitting up straight as an idea struck her, and her mind raced as she flicked through the pages, desperate to read more of her mother's wisdom, or any pointers that might help endure her absence.

Maybe this was *exactly* what was needed to mend things – something to gather up all the little broken pieces that were this family now, and help put them back together?

As Romy continued reading, something akin to hope blossomed within her for the first time all year, as she realised that this was the miracle she'd been searching for.

Thank you, Mum. I think I know what to do . . .

While this family might be sinking beneath the surface at the moment, perhaps, with a little guidance, there was hope for them yet.

END OF EXCERPT.

THE BEAUTIFUL LITTLE THINGS is out now in ebook, paperback and audio.

ABOUT THE AUTHOR

USA Today & international #1 bestselling author Melissa Hill lives in Dublin. Her page-turning contemporary stories are published worldwide and translated into 25 different languages.

Multiple titles are in development for movies and TV.

A GIFT TO REMEMBER is currently airing on Hallmark Channel US, or Sky Cinema in UK/Ireland and THE CHARM BRACELET film adaptation was released Christmas, 2020.

A movie of CHRISTMAS BENEATH THE STARS airs December 2021 in the US.

www.melissahill.ie

Printed in Great Britain
by Amazon